Blaze™

The White Star Continuity

Book 2

HIDDEN GEMS

by

Carrie Alexander

Jamie Wilson thinks his best friend,
Marissa Suarez, is dating the wrong men—and
his wanting her for himself has *nothing* to do with
his opinion. When Marissa's apartment suddenly
becomes a target for thieves, Jamie steps up to the
plate. Maybe Marissa will finally see the hidden
gem he is—inside the bedroom and out!

Book 3: CAUGHT by Kristin Hardy,
available March

Book 4: INTO TEMPTATION by Jeanie London,
available April

Book 5: FULL CIRCLE by Shannon Hollis,
available May

Book 6: DESTINY'S HAND by Lori Wilde,
available June

Blaze™

Dear Reader,

Welcome to Book 2 of THE WHITE STAR miniseries, where romantic legend and the battle between good and evil meet the contemporary sizzle of a Harlequin Blaze love story. What a treat it's been for me to work with the group of talented authors and editors who were involved in this project. I'm thrilled you're sharing the adventure with us!

My story is a light caper with a friends-to-lovers theme. I like a strong heroine, and Marissa Suarez is that: bold, confident and mouthy. Usually I'd match her up with an equally bold hero, but Marissa needed someone to trust. Someone like Jamie Wilson, the "boy next door." When a powerful amulet comes into their lives, along with threats and danger from all directions, Marissa learns that Jamie has been her hero all along.

Please enjoy their story. You can follow the twists and turns the amulet takes through the subsequent White Star books from Kristin Hardy, Jeanie London, Shannon Hollis and Lori Wilde. Visit my Web site at www.CarrieAlexander.com for contests, excerpts and more.

Best wishes,

Carrie Alexander

Books by Carrie Alexander

HARLEQUIN BLAZE

HIDDEN GEMS

Carrie Alexander

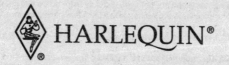

HARLEQUIN®

TORONTO • NEW YORK • LONDON
AMSTERDAM • PARIS • SYDNEY • HAMBURG
STOCKHOLM • ATHENS • TOKYO • MILAN • MADRID
PRAGUE • WARSAW • BUDAPEST • AUCKLAND

To Jennifer for being in my corner

With thanks to Kathryn for trusting me with her baby

ISBN 0-373-79240-9

HIDDEN GEMS

Copyright © 2006 by Carrie Antilla.

www.eHarlequin.com

Printed in U.S.A.

The Legend Continues...

Long ago and far away was an ancient kingdom where the desert and river intersected with the heavens. There lived a handsome young warrior named Egmath and his beloved, the princess Batu. Ever since the two were children, they had believed with all their hearts that they were destined to be together. Over the years they had often met in secret beneath the stars, sharing their dreams in whispers and innocent kisses.

But Egmath and Batu were soon separated. He went into training as a soldier in the king's army. She was tutored in the royal palace with her older sister, Anan. Both girls awaited the time that their father, the king, would arrange suitable marriages. Batu prayed daily that one day her hand would be given to Egmath.

The time came when a conflict arose between the small desert kingdom and a neighboring village. After several skirmishes, the king's army was victorious. Egmath returned as a hero, to be feted for his bravery with a grand party at the palace.

Egmath was eager to see Batu again, but his first respects must be paid to Anan. The princess was kind and comely, though lacking her younger sister's spirited beauty. The king looked on with approval.

Throughout the evening of dancing and music, Egmath had eyes only for Batu. She was exotic and glamorous in her finest gown and ornate jewels. As the night grew long, he spied her sneaking away through the small palace's stone courtyard and hurried to follow.

She went to their favorite meeting place, a lush copse near the river where the water pooled among mossy rocks. Egmath stopped and watched her, hidden by the palms as she stripped to a linen shift and dove into the water.

Alarmed, he emerged from the darkness. "Batu."

She swam to him through the gleaming dark green water.

"You should not be here alone." The words choked in his throat as she rose, slim and graceful, the shift clinging to her ripe curves. "You are a woman now, no longer a child."

Batu's eyes sparkled provocatively as she pressed water from her long black hair. "I am not alone as long as you are here."

He tapped the miniature pearl cat strung on a cord around her neck. "You still wear your amulet."

"Of course. I am not married yet." All youth wore the amulets, to be surrendered only when the boys became men and the girls became wives.

The mention of marriage gave Batu a strange shyness. When she looked into Egmath's eyes, her heartbeat skittered like a scorpion in the sand. He was so tall, his body grown strong and hard and unfamiliar.

She had to look away. They had been apart for too long.

"Batu, you must know how much I have missed you." He caught her chin, then touched his palm to her cheek. The kohl and bright paint had washed away from her eyes and lips. The fancy jewels were gone. She was still the girl he'd always loved.

Yet different. Desire burned within him.

She came into his arms. "Oh, Egmath. I was so afraid I would lose you."

"Never."

She lifted her face. "Promise me."

He responded without thinking, saying what he wanted to be true. "I promise, sweet one."

He touched a tender kiss to her lips, intending only to reassure her before they returned to the party. A warm breeze stirred the eucalyptus and acacia, bending the tips of the cypress trees. From the black desert, a jackal howled.

Egmath's blood quickened. He tightened his arms around Batu. The body that had been as slender and strong as a reed was now softer and rounded, inciting his hunger. Their kiss deepened, becoming passionate instead of chaste.

"Promise," Batu pleaded. Life was not as simple as it had been when they were children. She feared their future was uncertain despite a hundred promises from Egmath's lips.

Courting a thrilling danger, he boldly cupped her breast. His stroking fingers chased away her worry.

"We will be together forever," he vowed.

"Together forever," she agreed as the fire leaped between them.

She believed. Their love was as unrelenting as the wind that swept across the dunes, as constant as the flow of the river, as everlasting as the stars in the sky.

She would always believe.

TO BE CONTINUED...

1

"I HAVE NOTHING to declare," Marissa Suarez told the customs agent in a voice like broken glass, "except that my boyfriend's a swine."

A snicker rose from the crowded line behind her.

The bored official merely stamped her customs declaration form without looking up. "You can't bring pork products into the country, ma'am."

Marissa squinted. "Oh, don't worry. I left his bacon miles behind."

Paul Beckwith, forthwith known as Cheating Slime, was still in the Cayman Islands hobnobbing with his clients. If he'd missed Marissa it was only because she wasn't there to slather sunscreen on his perfectly trapezoid shoulders and back. But any bunny off the beach could handle *that* duty. Paul would have no objections. When he hadn't been ditching her for "vital" meetings, he'd been drooling over every pair of bouncing breast implants on Seven Mile beach.

Marissa Suarez was not a woman who put up with that kind of bullshit.

She was, unfortunately, a woman who chose the kind of man who shoveled it.

Every...damn...time.

With a clenched-teeth smile, she took the card from the customs official and tucked it into her passport. She truly had nothing to declare. Returning five days early from a supposedly romantic getaway, she was not only sans boyfriend, but minus the promised toasty tan and post-coital bliss, too.

However, she *had* acquired a resolution during the flight into JFK: no more bad choices, no more mistakes.

Next time—because, let's face it, she wasn't going to swear off men altogether—she would pick a guy who was the antithesis of the handsome, career-driven charmers she usually went for. Someone sweet, tender, laid-back.

So what if she wasn't sweet, tender or laid-back herself? Opposites were supposed to attract.

New arrivals jostled into the roped-off customs line. A fat woman with a bad sunburn and a floppy hat jarred Marissa's elbow just as she'd twisted to tuck her official papers into the straw bag hanging off her shoulder.

The documents flew from her hand. When she bent to reach for it, the woman beaned her in the head with a bulging carry-on.

Marissa bounced off the cordon and pitched forward in her spike-heeled sandals, falling onto her hands and knees. "Ouch!"

"Let me help," said a deep male voice. The French

accent seemed to be authentic, but in Marissa's current state of mind she was prone to doubt the sincerity of the entire male species. "These people have no manners."

The stranger knelt near her suitcase, smoothly offering one hand to help her stand while swooping up the passport with his other. He was dark and slight, with a seriously I'm-too-French-for-razors stubble happening below his gaunt cheekbones. He reeked of tobacco. Smoky sunglasses concealed his eyes, but she sensed he'd evaluated her in one lizard-like blink.

Marissa rose and brushed away the strands of hair that had come free of her ponytail. Her knees stung. "Thank you, but please let me have that," she said, being politely firm as she reached for her passport.

The Frenchman had maneuvered her around so that her back was to the bustling meet-and-greet area. His eyes crawled over her photo ID and return ticket. Marissa steeled herself to deflect a suave compliment on her ebony hair or exotic eyes—she'd heard them all—but he simply handed over the passport without comment.

After a glance past her shoulder, then the faintest twitch of a smile, he melted away into the nattering crowd of arrivals who'd cleared customs. "Good day."

Odd. Marissa snapped the passport shut and pressed it to her breastbone, feeling the way she did when a shadow passed over the sun. She checked her luggage, half expecting that he'd lifted her wallet. But all was intact, including the tagged and processed bag sitting at her feet.

"Outta my way, supermodel," said the fat woman in

a Bronx patois that hacksawed through the moment of unease. She trundled by with a large stack of luggage.

"Pardon," Marissa trilled. Thankful that she'd traveled light, she reached for the small suitcase that was packed with little more than damp bikinis, shorts, tanks and a couple of sundresses. The big straw carry-all she'd purchased on the island held a stash of Evian, her wallet and passport, makeup bag, camera, the current issue of French *Vogue* and five crumpled sheets of stationery from the Grand Cayman Beachcomber.

Paul—Sorry, but I'm leaving. I was annoyed when you abandoned me at the hotel bar, but to ditch

Paul,
Next time you invite a girlfriend on a business trip, don't claim it's a romantic getaway..

Dear Paul,
Clearly, we are not working out. It was a mistake to get involved in the first place, so I'm sure we can agree to pretend that this never hap

Dickhead—I'm so out of here!

Dear Paul—I've booked an earlier flight with my return ticket. First class. Don't worry, I paid the difference myself. Enjoy the rest of your midnight "business" meetings.
Your ex,
Marissa

THE FINAL VERSION of the letter was the one she'd stuck on the mirror in their suite, then removed at the last moment. She was better at face-to-face confrontation. But there'd been no time to wait around for that, and, anyway, he'd deserved to be left in the dark about her sudden departure.

She'd swept the wadded-up notes into her bag so he wouldn't find them, grabbed her swimsuits off the shower curtain rod and hurried to the lobby to catch the late airport shuttle. After making a couple of calls to friends to let them know she was on her way home, she'd turned off her cell phone for the duration of the trip.

She had no intention of listening to Paul's outrage at being left in the lurch. Recriminations weren't her thing. Neither was wallowing and weeping. She always recognized when a relationship was over and believed in lopping off dead meat with a quick, decisive cut.

Which would be much easier if she hadn't made the colossal mistake of hooking up with a workmate from Howard, Coffman, Ellis and Schnitzer, the Manhattan law firm where she'd been employed since graduation from Columbia Law. Fortunately, Paul would be even less inclined to bring their breakup into the office. She was still one of the multitude of associates, while he was on the fast track to junior partner. He had more to lose.

Marissa left the customs area and stepped sideways around a couple of city cops with radios clipped to their shoulders and holsters at their hips. They were coordinating with an airport official and his uniformed security staff, passing out photocopies of a suspect's mug shot.

Uh-oh. Security sweep. Get a move on.

Marissa slipped in and out of the crowds of huggers and criers, still worrying about her job. She'd known it was a foolish move to get involved with Paul, yet she'd done it anyway. Even in the early days of the romance, when he was charming and attentive and neither of them had been thinking of practical matters, she hadn't expected to avoid office gossip entirely. The legal secretaries always knew which of the firm's employees were getting their briefs filed, even when the senior partners were oblivious.

Worse, she couldn't blame Paul for the bad decision. *She'd* made the choice. *She'd* believed he was worth a risk. *She'd* believed maybe this time…

"When will I ever learn?" she muttered, digging into the straw bag to find her cell. She flipped it open and checked her messages, dodging an overzealous gypsy cabdriver who tried to snag her arm.

Four messages from Paul. She got a petty but satisfying spurt of retribution by deleting them with a punch of her thumb.

She almost bumped into a young woman in religious sect garb: head kerchief and a plain calf-length dress with a white collar and black stockings. The girl turned, smiled modestly and offered Marissa a bloom from the bucket of daisies and tulips at her feet.

A pure white Stargazer lily.

"Beautiful," Marissa said, surprised. Even though she didn't usually slow for hucksters, she dug into the straw bag and pulled a five out of her wallet.

"Blessings on you." The young lady nodded. "May you find true love."

"Yes, here's to love." Marissa meant to be sarcastic, but no conviction remained. Although coming home early was a smart step, she would have to continue traveling in a new direction if she hoped to find true love.

Ah, but did she? That was a question to ponder. *Not* looking for love wasn't working. How likely was it that she'd have any luck if her expectations were even higher?

Juggling the phone, she tucked the lily behind her ear, then returned to her messages. One was from her mother in Miami, who had the notion that any time Marissa flew over Florida she should stop in to say hello, as if the airlines issued parachutes along with packets of stale peanuts.

The last message put a smile on Marissa's face. Jamie Wilson. Her best friend, guy version. If there was anyone who could untwist her insides and aim her in the right direction, it was Jamie. She speed-dialed him.

He answered on the first ring. "Where are you, babe?"

"Back on U.S. soil. Making my way to the taxi lane." Jamie was the only man she let call her "babe." From a snake like Paul, the pet name would ooze with condescension. From Jamie, it was about cozy familiarity, as if they were an old married couple who finished each other's thoughts. Which they almost were. Jamie was the straight Will to her Grace, proof that men and women truly could be "just" friends.

"Did you practice your yoga breathing on the plane

like I said?" Jamie was always telling her she needed to slow her usual pace—full speed ahead.

"With a carpet salesman from Jersey and his horking wife at my elbow? Not a chance. But after the attendant had removed the airsick bags, I did wind down with one of those itty-bitty bottles of rum."

"You'll be dehydrated then."

"I know. Want to meet me for drinks? Maybe a little cheese with my whine?"

"How about actual food?"

"I guess." Her stomach was hollow, but she was too hyper to eat. Normally she'd channel her energy into a good workout—either at the gym or in the bedroom— but that was out for the time being. Tomorrow, she'd get back on the treadmill, literally and figuratively. If she never found an appropriate man, at least she'd qualify for the fitness Olympics.

"I need to stop by home first to dump my luggage," she said, tugging at the shoulder strap of the suitcase. "Meet you there." Jamie lived upstairs from her, in a vintage brownstone in the Village.

"Where are you now?" he asked.

She glanced up. "Almost to the exit. If the taxi line isn't too long, I'll be in the city by—"

"Turn left," Jamie said.

"But—"

"Just do it."

Because it was Jamie, she obeyed, making such an abrupt detour she almost tripped over the trolley of

Louis Vuitton cases a chauffeur was wielding like a feed store wheelbarrow.

Jamie appeared out of the moving crowd, cell phone at his ear.

"You dork," she said, blinking back the moisture that sprang to her eyes. "I told you not to go to the trouble of meeting me."

"Hey, a vacation breakup deserves an airport pick up. It's synergy." He dropped the phone into the pocket of his baggy khakis and put his arms around her. "I'm only sorry I couldn't find a car to borrow. We'll have to get a taxi."

She pressed her face into his shoulder, just for a moment or two. Three, four, five. Her heart surged with gratitude. He felt as warm and comforting as ever, but also muscled and solid. When had that happened?

He'd been a skinny dude with an unintentionally hip geekiness when they'd met three years ago while playing Ultimate Frisbee with a group of friends in the park. In between putting in eighty hours a week at work, she'd been dating one of her typical Mr. Right Turn To Disasters. Jamie had been seeing her ex-roomie, self-proclaimed bitch diva goddess Shandi Lee—an odd couple if ever there was one. The relationships had lasted just long enough for Marissa and Jamie to avoid the awkward "should they or shouldn't they?" moment and settle into platonic friendship.

Lucky timing, Marissa had always thought. Jamie Wilson had become the only long-term chromosome XY in her day-to-day life, the only male, aside from her cat, Harry, that she wasn't pressured to impress.

"Marissa," he said, patting her back. "I'm sorry."

She squeezed him, allowing his sympathy even though too much sentiment usually made her itchy and restless. Outside of the holidays, when she was a sap about family cheer and goodwill to men, she kept her game face on. A single woman in Manhattan had to be tough.

And yet once again she felt herself relaxing into Jamie's patented comfort zone, the one place where she let down her guard. He felt strong. He smelled good. Not like Paul, granted, who'd given off the alpha wolf eat-or-be-eaten pheromones that typically revved her engine. But surprisingly good, all the same.

Surprisingly sexy for a best friend.

What? Her head cranked back.

Beep, beep, beep. Time to back up that truck before it drove over the cliff looming ahead.

"Enough of this. I'm not *dying*." Marissa pulled out of Jamie's arms. "It's just another breakup. I've survived them before." She tucked away the cell phone that was still clutched in her hand, watching his face through her lashes while she snapped the bag shut.

Jamie seemed unaware of her instant of sexual awareness. He looked the way he always did—strong nose and jaw, blunt cheekbones, big dark blue eyes with sleepy lids beneath the mop of nut-brown hair that fell across his brow. A mouth so mobile that she'd learned to read his emotions from the shapes it made.

At the moment he was holding a faintly quizzical smile, his expression as clear and innocent as a choir boy's. No sign of any of the messy, secret yearnings she'd occasionally worried he might harbor for her, that Shandi, among others, had sworn were there.

Who knew that Marissa, the tough *chiquita* from the barrio, would crack first?

She shrugged. Well, whatever had happened was only a momentary weakness. Gone like a speeding bullet, she told herself, although an alarming amount of warmth toward Jamie still simmered inside her.

Ignore it. No more mistakes, remember?

"You okay?" he asked, taking her rare uncertainty for Paul Beckwith aftereffects.

"Sure." She tossed her ponytail. "You know me. Paul's roadkill in my rearview mirror."

"But this time, you'll have to keep seeing him." Jamie had warned her not to have a workplace affair. He was always so sensible, telling her in his evenhanded way exactly what was wrong with the man she'd chosen. That he was invariably right but never said "I told you so" was one of his most endearing characteristics.

. Which didn't mean she'd ever learn to listen to him! But it was nice having someone looking out for her.

"Not to worry," she said. "We're both too busy for office drama."

"If you say so." He scowled as he took her bag.

"Now, Jamie. I only need one stern *papi* and I left *him* behind in Little Havana." Jamie's brotherly concern was nowhere near as stifling as the concern of Alberto Suarez, an old-fashioned Cuban American who thought that his eldest daughter should be married and popping out babies like a good little Catholic. Two years shy of thirty and she was already considered an old maid by her family. "So don't look at me like that."

Jamie blinked. "Like what?"

"Like you know what's best for me." She kissed his cheek. Another tingle of awareness chased itself over the surface of her skin, which she continued to ignore. Jet lag could knock anyone off center.

"Someone has to," he teased. His eyes went to the lily in her hair.

She touched it, feeling an emotion so rare she almost didn't recognize it. *Shyness.*

"You look very tropical." His voice rasped.

"Even without the tan I was promised?" She made a face. "Instead of lying on the beach, most of my time in the Caymans was wasted holed up in the suite or hanging around the bar, waiting for Paul."

"That doesn't sound like you."

"Exactly. Once I realized that, I made my escape." They walked through the exit doors. She scanned the cordoned taxi line, dismayed to see that it would be another wait for transportation. "Men don't treat me that way more than once."

"Like what, specifically?"

Marissa gave a snort. "Like an accessory."

Her father had attempted to raise her to be what he considered a "good" girl—obedient and humble. Obviously that lesson hadn't taken, perhaps because he'd also taught her pride and pugnacity by example. Instead of accepting a gender role, she'd preferred to outdo his expectations for the boys in the family, even when that meant working as a waitress to put herself through the first years of community college, even when she was told over and over that she would never make it.

The desire to achieve a success that would show them all what she was made of had become her driving force. She couldn't be like her cheery, tolerant mother, née Mary Margaret McBride, who was content in her little cottage, still in love with her bantam rooster of a husband after thirty-two years of marriage. Or her sister, Graciela, who'd married at twenty and now had a husband who spent more evenings out drinking with his *muchachos* than at home with his family.

Marissa appreciated her parents for the stability and love they'd given her and her brothers and sister. But she'd known from the age of ten that she had to be aggressive or she'd never get away. If she was single-minded and frequently too abrupt, that was why.

Until she was where she wanted to be, she couldn't let up. She couldn't slow down.

Except with Jamie. He was her release valve, as she was his energy pill. They went together like salt and pepper, up and down, yin and yang. Each gave as good as they got, and it worked.

"An accessory?" Jamie had to know there was more to her early return than that, but he wasn't one to push. "For a smart man, Paul sure is dumb," he said cheerfully. "You're a treasure."

Marissa shook her head. "I'm a woman in need of a giant *Cubano* sandwich." Suddenly she was starving.

"Then let's get out of here so I can feed you," Jamie

said, reverting to the reliable friend she recognized. They'd reached the head of the line and he'd stashed her suitcase in their taxi's trunk. He held the door open, smiling at her, adorably rumpled in a tee layered over a white cotton shirt with frayed edges. No fashion plate, her friend, Jamie. Nothing like Paul, who spent more on his wardrobe than many women.

Marissa climbed into the taxi. After she was settled, she took a moment to thank her lucky stars for the Frisbee she'd mistakenly aimed at Jamie's nose the day they'd met. She was certain that he'd never once thought of her as an accessory, even though she'd been his plus one at a number of the events that he attended in his career as an arts writer for the *Village Observer,* a smallish daily newspaper targeted at the city's trendy, upscale culture vultures.

No. To Jamie, she really was a treasure.

The surprise for her was in realizing how mutual the sentiment had become.

JEAN LUC ALLARD had given the officials the slip. Child's play, he thought as he slithered through the throng near the airport exit, though in fact he'd narrowly escaped the wide net cast by the cops and security guards that had swarmed the JFK terminal.

He'd skipped out of the boarding area in the nick of time, then taken the long detour through Arrivals to avoid crossing under their noses. But they'd also covered that area.

An unpleasant surprise. One that had forced him into ditching the goods despite the huge risk that entailed.

After making his move, he'd managed to reach a rest room, where he'd switched his dark glasses and leather jacket with the Patriots jersey and baseball cap stowed in his bag. The fake French passport he'd booked his tickets under was lodged in the crevice behind one of the sinks, replaced with an American one that claimed he was Joe Martin from Stonington, Massachusetts.

The risk made Allard's gut churn. Fortunately he'd planned for all eventualities. But how had the bastards known where to find him in the first place?

A lucky tip from an informant…or a double cross?

Unlikely. He'd had contact with no one except his employer, a wealthy European with a large bank account and a larger ego. Allard had a number to call when he reached the rendèzvous point, and no more.

He was on his own. As he preferred. His father had taught him to trust no one.

Even in the innocuous getup, passersby gave the Frenchman's black scowl a wide berth. He paid them little heed, consumed by his racing thoughts. There would be no mercy with a fortune at stake. He would cut the throat of any person who dared stop him.

Already he had left one body behind. He'd cold-cocked an interloper outside the ransacked safe of Stanhope's Auction House, snatching the prize from the man's hands even as he'd crumpled to the floor. Naturally, the theft of late heiress Zoey Zander's vast collection of jewels had made the news. Every thief of international repute was reported to be a suspect.

While the New York police had paddled in place,

squabbling with Interpol like ducks on the Seine, Allard had bided his time in a nondescript Brooklyn hotel room. Once he'd believed the stateside situation had cooled down, he'd booked a ticket to the Buenos Aires drop point.

To be thwarted now made his blood thin with displeasure. *Merde!* He'd been one boarding pass away from his escape.

That he'd become the security agent's quarry was not in question. What remained to be seen was if they'd realized that the heist had been arranged solely to acquire the White Star, an ivory amulet so rare and revered that few had known of its existence until the auction house had publicized the contents of the Zander estate.

For these past weeks, he—and he alone—had owned the White Star. Caressed her. Held her to his lips in defiance of the legend she carried, which prophesied love for the pure of heart, a cursed future for all else.

And now she was gone.

Though Allard's face betrayed no emotion, his tongue was bitter with frustration.

He spat. *Pah.*

The anxious officials' presence had prevented him from boarding the flight to South America. He'd been cornered like a rodent, forced to take an incredible risk. Getting caught with the amulet was not an option. Therefore, regrettably, the White Star was no longer in his possession.

An extreme nuisance, that, but a necessity under the circumstances.

Carefully positioned out of the bustle, but close enough to move fast when need be, Allard cupped his hand to light a cigarette. He leaned against the building, dragging on the stinging taste of tobacco. Behind the sunglasses, his eyes zipped back and forth between the herds of American travelers, most of them waiting patiently in line like cows.

Ah, there she was.

Marissa Suarez. Stunning girl, with silken black hair and legs that went forever. It might be amusing to prolong his surveillance and seduce his way into her apartment rather than resort to the usual break-in. His employer would not approve of the indiscretion, but the man seemed to have a talent for buffing his nails while subordinates accomplished his dirty work.

Allard didn't mind. He excelled in living on the fly, taking advantage of opportunities that presented themselves.

Smoke curled from his nostrils. Covertly he studied the girl. She was smart, aware of her surroundings, holding her straw bag close to her body while she waited at the curb. The man who had met her inside kept a firm grip on the other bag.

Allard saw he had no choice. An immediate recovery attempt was too risky. Not only were there authorities in the vicinity, but the girl could identify his face, particularly if he attracted more attention to himself.

He should have chosen a less observant mark, one of the weary tourists with their heaps of mismatched baggage. All too stupid to realize what he'd planted on them. But this one had literally fallen at his feet.

The boyfriend put his hand at her back, guiding her into a cab. The vital suitcase had gone into the trunk.

Allard ground the cigarette beneath his heel. He smiled to himself, pleased by his maneuvers. The unfortunate situation was under control. While his employer would be enraged if he knew the treasure had been out of Allard's hands for even a minute, the man need only be told of the unavoidable delay of their rendezvous. Let him sputter and squawk. In the end, he would wait.

As would Allard. For a million euros, he could put up with any annoyance, any delay. He was beholden only to the White Star.

A sharp whistle summoned one of the gypsy cabs. He slid inside and mumbled a directive to the driver around the fresh cigarette he'd inserted in his mouth. As the vehicle pulled away, two of the security guards emerged from the terminal, their frustration as evident as their empty hands.

Smirking, Allard slunk low in the back seat while the car neatly whisked him away from beneath the officials' noses. He'd escaped unscathed once more.

2

MARISSA YAWNED and leaned her head on Jamie's shoulder. "How come we've never had sex?" she said with a throaty giggle, snuggling up to him in their favorite carved wooden booth at Havana Eva de Cuba, where he'd been plying her with carbohydrates instead of alcohol.

Jamie dragged in a deep breath before draping an arm around her. He was too nice for his own good. *Definitely* too nice.

"I mean, it would be so easy," she continued, her voice muffled by his chest. He had to lean his head closer to hear her over the din of the busy and colorful restaurant, a frequent hangout only two blocks from their apartment building. Marissa liked the place for the ethnic menu and decor that reminded her of home, not that she'd ever admit to such sentimental longings.

As for Jamie, he'd go anywhere she did.

"I know *you* wouldn't hurt me when we broke up," she finished. "And then we could still stay friends."

Since she'd spent the past ninety minutes telling him and her girlfriends that she wasn't hurt by Paul's betrayal, the first part of the statement was more revealing than she intended.

He touched his nose and lips to her hair, hurting for her more than she'd ever hurt for herself. Marissa pained him, she frustrated him, she exhilarated him. He'd wanted her from the day they met, but now wasn't the time to take her question seriously. "Why would you want to start something with the intention of breaking up?"

"Not an intention. A given." She tilted her face up, lightly knocking her forehead against his chin. Her lids were weighted and she had the dopey, slightly boozy grin that meant she was about fifteen minutes from crashing. "I'm a realist. There's always a breakup."

"Only because you choose the wrong men."

She sighed and snuggled back in. He felt a shiver pass through her slender body. "We've already established that there's something off about my taste in men. And since I agree that I've got to stop doing this to myself, next time I need to find a nice guy. Like you." After a moment—Jamie was sure only he felt the strain of it—she chuckled. "But of course not you."

Of course not. He looked at the tin ceiling. At least she still remembered there was a possibility of their having got together at some point. Perhaps he hadn't wandered so deep into the "just friends" zone that there was no coming back.

Three years he'd known her. Three years waiting for the right time to tell her that he thought there could be more than friendship between them. First, there'd been other people in their lives. Then, for a long time, he'd convinced himself that she was hopelessly out of his league—a savvy, single-minded attorney who worked and played among the upper strata wouldn't be interested in an easygoing arts writer who counted his dog among his best friends. So he'd kept his interest buried beneath layers of playing the good guy and best friend. Told himself he was better off that way, since Marissa lost her good sense when it came to her love life. He didn't want to be one of her regrets. To say nothing of losing her as a friend.

Cassandra Richards returned from the ladies' room to lean over the table. She was part of Marissa's circle of friends, a stunning blonde who worked in fashion, in some sort of public relations capacity. The type of woman who, with one flick of her lashes, could make Jamie feel like a teenager again—all ears, nose, big feet and gangly limbs. He frequently found himself wondering how a brainy boy from the Connecticut suburbs had wound up associating with such Manhattan beauties. If his teenage garage band could see him now…

"How's our girl?" Cass asked. She had dropped by to lend her support, even though Marissa had been adamant about how very okay she was without Paul… while downing *mojitos,* one right after the other, before the food had arrived.

Eyes shut, Marissa aimed a sleepy smile at her friend. "Drifting."

Cass sent her wry look Jamie's way. "Finally."

Marissa's index finger twitched. "You go home. I've kept you too long."

"I'll hold your hair anytime, Mari."

Marissa grinned at the girlfriend shorthand for their mutual support system. She pressed a hand to her stomach. "No literal pilgrimages to the porcelain goddess tonight, please."

Jamie rubbed her back, hoping for the same. He'd hold back her hair, but not if that made him one of the girls.

"Time to take her home," he said to Cassandra, who'd arrived in a slouchy sweater with her whisper-fine hair tucked haphazardly in a clip. She still managed to look like a princess among the paupers.

"Need any help?"

"Thanks, I've got her."

Cass snapped open her bag and dropped several bills on the table to pay for a share of the drinks, sandwiches and *très leches*. She'd matured from the last time Jamie had seen her. According to Marissa, Cass had fallen under the good influence of a cop from Queens. That sounded like a strange pairing to Jamie, but he'd taken it as a sign of hope for himself.

"Great," Cass said, "because I've got work in the morning, unlike Happy Holidays here. I need to get home."

"Hold on." Jamie made a motion to slide out of the booth. Marissa tried to straighten up, not very successfully. "I'll walk you to the train."

"Nonsense. It's not that far to Tribeca. I'll grab a cab." Cass leaned down and pecked Marissa's flushed cheek. "Call you tomorrow."

"Mmm-hmm."

"Take care." Cass gave Jamie an appreciative smile.

The luggage they'd stored under the table caught her eye as she turned to leave. "Don't forget the bags."

"Nothing important in 'em," Marissa murmured. "Just my broken dreams."

Jamie waved a couple of fingers at Cass before turning his attention back to the woman tucked beneath his arm. Marissa, she of the sharp angles and razor tongue, wasn't warm and cuddly very often. Was it wrong to enjoy the hell out of holding her this way when she was only looking for a friendly shoulder?

"Also your passport and credit cards and house keys," he said, nudging the suitcase with his toe.

"Gawd, I've become maudlin." Her face scrunched in revulsion. "That means it's abs'lutely, positively time to go."

"Are you up to walking?"

"Sure. I'm not drunk. Only kind of loose." She let her arms flop.

Like a broken doll, Jamie thought, knowing that tomorrow she would be a warrior woman again. Tonight there was a rather large chink in her armor. If ever he'd have the chance to explore her feelings for him…

But he couldn't take advantage. Not because he was all that noble. Because she'd be miffed with him tomorrow, and Marissa in a temper brought even more of his hidden feelings to the surface. Her passion had always awed him. Although he'd tried to keep himself at arm's length at the start of their friendship, he'd been a moth to her intense flame. No way could he maintain a distance, even when that meant going home singed by her lack of awareness. He told himself that while being her lover would be incredible, having her as a friend was enough.

Jamie hesitated. He'd lied. Friendship wasn't enough. Besides, *she'd* brought up the question, not him. But he'd like an answer.

Why *hadn't* they ever hooked up?

Marissa spoke first. "I'm sorry I've been so needy. You probably had better things to do this evening."

"Not at all." He had a movie review to write, but that wasn't due until eleven tomorrow morning. Plenty of time, especially since he'd be up all night, taming tonight's wayward urges. Marissa had no idea what he suffered for her.

"Ready to go?"

"I guess." She slid out of the booth.

"Wait here." He went to pay the bill to speed up the process, idling for a few minutes in the throng around the cash register. He watched the dark glimmer of Marissa's reflection in the mirror behind the bar. She stared blankly across the room. Vulnerability was evident in her unschooled expression, and he nearly groaned out loud at the rare sight.

Oh, hell. He couldn't press her tonight. She needed a white knight. That would be him—again.

She was squinting into the crowd when he returned. He asked her what she was looking for and got a shrug. "Thought I saw someone from the airport."

"Not Paul."

"Course not. He's still in the Caymans, having *meetings.*"

Jamie handed her the straw purse, then dragged the lightweight suitcase out from beneath the table. "Are you ever going to tell me exactly what happened there?" A chattering group pushed past them to claim the table.

"It's so predictable." Marissa took a big breath when they emerged onto the street. "I hate being predictable."

The night air was cool and fresh, a rarity that was unique to a few brief weeks of spring in the city. After the long winter, the Village had burst into life, throbbing with the beating drums of meeting, teasing, making love, making mistakes. Or maybe it was just Jamie's head screwing with him because that was all that he could think about, especially since Marissa had brought up the subject of sex.

They headed toward the crosswalk onto Bleecker Street. "C'mon, tell me the story," Jamie said. "I need to know whether or not I have to beat up Paul." The statement was sure to get a laugh, given his resident pet geek status.

Marissa didn't laugh. She peered at him from the corners of her eyes for a full five seconds before her berry-ripe lips stretched into an amused smile. "Thanks, darling. I'll just kick Paul in the family jewels if he ever approaches me again."

"Ow."

She took his hand, twining their arms and swinging them as they walked. The cool air had perked her up. "Paul and I had been falling apart even before the Caymans. The trip was a last-ditch effort to keep the romance going." Her face went grim. "If it was ever a romance at all."

"I thought that Paul had swept you off your feet." Hearing the details of their fancy dinners with champagne and roses had eaten Jamie up inside.

"Yes, well, turns out that I've been deceiving myself about what we meant to each other. After the first flush of attraction, we had nothing in common except ambition." She squeezed Jamie's fingers. "That's always my mistake. I go for the flashy dressings when what I need is a man of real substance."

What she needed was to figure out why she was drawn to the wrong men when she knew she'd end up unsatisfied. He'd recognized the pattern four disastrous relationships ago.

"What did Paul do?"

"I'm more unhappy with myself than him." She wrinkled her nose. "But it was like I said. He promised me a fabulous spring vacation in the Caribbean. Then when we got there I found out he'd actually set up meetings with clients. The Cayman Islands have advantageous offshore investment and banking regulations. We have several clients who've incorporated their businesses there to avoid taxes."

"Isn't that kind of shady?"

"Not really," she defended. "The law is the law. Howard, Coffman is a reputable firm." A frown crossed her face. "I'll admit I became curious about what Paul was up to. But when I asked to come along, he told me to get out of his business and into a bikini."

"Ah." Jamie almost smiled. He'd known the arrogant Paul would shoot himself in the foot sooner or later.

"Yeah. You know I hate getting that head-patting thing from guys. He tried to make it up to me when he came back, but I wasn't having any. After that, it was all downhill. He ditched me in the hotel bar and took calls the one time we actually made it to the beach."

She stopped, shook her head, then resumed a faster pace as they turned onto their home street, a short, narrow lane lined with chestnut trees and brownstones that had gone dark and quiet. "Enough. Let's just get home. I'm boring even myself with this rehashing."

"He hurt you. I can see it." Jamie was agitated because he knew Marissa was leaving something out. It wasn't like her to be evasive.

She turned quiet, firming her soft mouth as she stared straight ahead. Their footsteps echoed. "He cheated, okay? He said he had one last late-night meeting, and I guess that much was true because I saw him through my—"

She shot a shamefaced look at Jamie. "I didn't mean to spy. I'd been snapping photos of the sunset from the hotel balcony. I happened to spot Paul through the lens, a short way down the road outside a beachfront bar. He was talking to a man with a briefcase, so I didn't think too much of it until this island hoochie-coochie came up."

Marissa was absorbed in the story now. They'd slowed to a stop near the wide front steps of a stately brownstone with double oak doors, half a block from home. Jamie put the bag down and took her other hand.

She gave him a chagrined grin. "You know the type. Semi-pro. Big bleached-blond hair, implants, pink lipstick, high heels. I thought she was with Paul's client because he kissed her hello, but then she attached herself to Paul. And he was willing."

"You saw all of this through the camera?"

"Yes. I even—" She cut off. "It's so tawdry." She inched closer to Jamie. "The melodrama revolts me. I don't want that kind of life."

He knew why. She'd told him of the soap opera of life in Little Havana, where everyone had an opinion on each other's business, and how she'd escaped by keeping herself aloof and focused.

One of his hands went to her back, sliding up and down in a soothing caress while he struggled with the urge to take her into his arms, to hold her, love her, give her the closeness that she didn't know she desired. The hell of it was that even if she opened up her heart, the need for intimacy might *never* include him.

He cleared the knot in his throat. "Then what do you want?"

"I should want an average guy. Someone who spends the night. If he sneaks out the next morning, it's to bring me back the Sunday paper and coffee and muffins instead of going to the gym to perfect his physique."

Jamie wondered when she'd realize she'd described him, aside from the part about spending the night. Given her earlier question, maybe she already had. "You've thought this out."

Her head angled back, tilting her face toward his so that he was staring into her eyes. Beautiful olive eyes struck with shards of amber, gleaming like gems he could only admire from afar. Her lips parted.

"This is crazy," she said. "But ever since the airport, I've been wondering if maybe you…"

Jamie's head roared like a blast furnace. She didn't mean—she couldn't be saying—

"You and me," she blurted. "What if we, you know, tried it out to see? No drama. Just one kiss? In case we're missing out on something that could be really fantastic."

He spoke very slowly. "You're not thinking straight."

"Straight's done me no good so far."

"What about tomorrow?"

"Let's not think about that." Marissa reached up to brush her knuckles along his jaw. She rubbed, sliding her fingers to his chin, then his lips. Outlining them. "I want to know what it's like to kiss you." His lower lip rolled under her caress. "Haven't you ever wondered…"

He couldn't deny that. "Hell, yeah," he said, and suddenly he was kissing her the way he'd dreamed of a thousand times.

Except that he'd made all the right moves in his fantasies. This was real. It was their noses bumping until they got the right angle, it was worrying if he had garlic breath, it was the sudden jolt of electric sensation when their tongues touched, making their teeth clash. She'd opened her mouth before he was prepared.

But it was also Marissa, her body familiar in his arms. The scent of her, rich and arousing. The night air that had seemed so cool had become hot, vibrant with the promise of a glorious discovery.

She moved against him, arching her body so that he felt her breasts, making an urging sound at the back of her throat—as if he needed to be encouraged. This time he was the one to deepen the kiss when he stroked his tongue inside her mouth.

Marissa pulled back. She looked at him with rounded eyes. "What do you think?"

"I think that was amazing," he said in a raw whisper, unable to resist bringing his mouth down on hers again. The first kiss had been a shock, a mind-blowing assault on the senses. He wanted to try her again, taste her, with a thinking brain this time.

She resisted for a moment, then gave in with a low, inviting moan. Her lips opened to the first flick of his tongue. Her mouth was hot, salty. And so sweet.

This is right.

His palms stroked up and down her arms before locking on her hips, fingers spreading across her tight little ass and pressing her hips snug against his. Their heights were close, and her legs long enough to make up the small difference. Their bodies were in perfect alignment. All the appropriate parts matched up. The soft weight of her breasts pressed to his chest, the long, lean curves of her waist and hips melding to his lower body, where the hard bulge of his erection sought her warm hollow. He wanted to press further into her, he wanted the hot wet clasp, the intimate connection of a complete joining.

So much for the thinking brain. He was operating on pure animal need.

At first, the small noises of a pedestrian approaching barely penetrated his consciousness. Not until he felt a body stealthily brush by did he realize that something was wrong.

"Hey, you!" Jamie whirled around, wrenching Marissa out of his arms with more force than he intended. She cried out, stumbling toward the curb as she lost her balance. He turned back to grab her by the elbow, seeing that she was set safely on her feet before he went to confront the stranger.

His instincts had been right. The man had targeted the suitcase on the stoop, crouching low as if he was about to snatch it.

Jamie made a desperate lunge to yank the bag free. Doing so was easier than he'd expected. The thief hadn't gotten much of a hold.

With a yell, Jamie toppled over backward, the bag clasped in his arms. The other man didn't make another attempt, only raced off without a backward glance.

Jamie was stunned. Like most New Yorkers, he'd been confronted on the streets by a few crazies. But he'd never experienced a mugging, even in snatch-and-run style.

And so he was surprised by his reaction. Adrenaline had pumped through his body, shooting him full of aggression and bravado. He was a pacifist, and yet suddenly he *wanted* to fight.

Marissa knelt at his side, filled with feminine concern. "Are you all right? You took a hard fall."

Jamie put a hand to the gritty sidewalk as he found his breath. "Sure. Are you?"

"Yes. It was only—" She glanced over the empty

street. "Only a pitiful attempt at a mugging. Not even an armed one." She made a dismissive sound, but her voice was shaky. "Takes more 'n that to scare a couple of tough New Yorkers, right?"

Jamie set her suitcase on the sidewalk and jumped to his feet. He was charged, ready to chase down the itchy-fingered stranger. But the would-be mugger had vanished like smoke.

Jamie moved restlessly up and down off the curb, sucking air through his nose. "Did you get a look at him?"

"No. I was trying not to land in the gutter."

"He wore a hood," Jamie remembered. "He was about five-eight or nine. Skinny. I didn't really see his face."

"Should we call the cops?"

After a moment of consideration, they looked at each other and shrugged. Not worth the time and trouble, especially when the theft hadn't been successful. "Let's just get home," Marissa said with a quiet voice. "This has been a helluva day."

Of course. She had to be burned out. Jamie wrapped his arms around her. "Poor baby."

She hugged him tight. "Is this a good idea?"

"What?" He jerked away. Was she afraid he wanted to take up where they'd been interrupted? He did, of course, but that wasn't his first priority. Only the second through tenth.

"Distracting ourselves." She averted her face. "Inviting another mugging."

"Yeah, right. We should go." God only knew that if he started kissing her again, a tornado could whirl up around them and he wouldn't notice until they'd landed in Oz.

He left his arm around her the rest of the way home, whether or not she wanted the protection. She didn't demur, but stayed tucked under his wing, now and then leaning her head on his shoulder and letting out a very quiet sigh.

He remained hyperalert to every sound and motion up and down the street. His body thrummed with excess energy, but he kept that under wraps as best as he could. Strange how the surging endorphins produced by the theft attempt and their astonishing kisses were so much alike. He suspected that something had been kick-started inside him. And he was damned if he'd go back, even if that were possible.

When they arrived at their brownstone, he took charge with the keys and luggage. "I'm going to collapse," Marissa announced at her apartment door, forestalling him even before he attempted to get inside.

He tried not to let it bother him that she was so certain about ending their experiment that she'd given him not even the smallest opening to delay. "Let me check the place out," he said, sliding past her without waiting for permission. What the hell. He turned on lights, glancing into the bath and bedroom, even her closet. Every room was in its usual state—topsy-turvy. Housekeeping was not one of Marissa's talents.

"Find anything?" she called in a tone that said he was being overprotective.

"Hold on." He swept aside a lace curtain and tested

the window that opened onto the fire escape off the bedroom. More of the lace was draped over the bed. The faded rose wallpaper, white iron bed, scattered clothes, shoes and books gave the bedroom the look of an over-turned Victorian wastebasket.

"It pays to be cautious," he said, leaving the doors open behind him. "You've been gone for three days."

"Is that all?" She blinked at her living room as if it were a street person's cardboard box. Her shoulders were slumped. "I thought it was longer."

Marissa rarely drooped. Jamie wanted to bust Paul for doing that to her, but he had to keep it cool or she'd know how deep his feelings truly ran. "You're done in."

She took one look at his face and moved away, masking the rebuff by lifting her arms and rubbing at the back of her neck. Avoiding looking at him again.

"I'll be right back," he said.

He returned a minute later to find her curled up in her comfy armchair, her head tipping over. He dropped her cat into her lap. She said, "Oh-hh, Harry," and clutched the beloved pet to her chest so gratefully that he couldn't stay irked by her wordless withdrawal.

"Thank you for taking care of my kitty while I was gone," she said, practically purring herself as she rubbed cheeks with the blue-eyed Angora. They were a pair— pampered, elegant, aloof, but affectionate under the right circumstances. "You're too good to us."

Too good? Jamie shoved his hands in his pockets so he wouldn't touch her.

Too bad.

THREE A.M. on the fire escape outside of the apartment of Marissa Suarez, and Allard was huddled against the cold drip of a misty rain. The shallow warmth of the day had dissipated from the building's stones hours ago. He huffed a breath into his turned-up collar to warm his face. Patience and precision were a thief's stock in trade. Acting rashly was never wise.

A droplet fell off the tip of his nose. His mouth puckered. Resorting to an attempted snatch on the street had been a foolish mistake. He'd been seduced by the couple's distraction into thinking he could slip the amulet from the bag before they realized what was happening.

Flimsy as it was, the plan had almost worked. The alluring White Star had been at his fingertips when Marissa's boyfriend had torn the bag away.

A switchblade had waited in Allard's pocket, but he'd chosen to run. Better to escape than to risk a struggle and possible identification. There would be other opportunities.

He shifted into a squat and peered through the window. Dark and quiet inside. Marissa was sprawled on the bed, her white, long-haired cat a huddled lump on her chest. The feline's eyes shone at Allard, freezing his hand on the windowsill. He hated pets, cats especially. They were unpredictable creatures. One loud meow at the wrong moment and the girl might be jarred out of her sleep.

Allard tilted his head. There was the bag. He'd watched as a lethargic Marissa had lugged the suitcase into the bedroom and dropped it on the floor. He'd been prepared to intervene should she discover the treasure he'd hidden inside, but his luck had held. She hadn't bothered to unpack. Instead she'd given the thing a kick to shove it under her bed.

One corner stuck out, tempting him.

The window was locked. He was certain that he could get in after a bit of jimmying. Hadn't he already bypassed high-tech security systems in his quest for the White Star?

But there was the cat.

The damn cat. His nemesis. Allard's father, a minor thief and total asshole, had taught him that the smallest detail, if overlooked, could ultimately exact the greatest cost. Yet when he'd seen his son's irrational fear of cats, he'd sneeringly called Jean *La Souri Noire*—the dark mouse—on their midnight excursions. To this day, he believed cats were bad luck.

The feline watched Allard, twitching its fluffy tail. After a moment of debate, he eased away from the window. For now, the White Star was safe.

Unlike his drunken lout of a father, he was a patient man. He would watch and wait for his next chance and when it came, he would be ready.

Not even the cat would prevent his fated reunion with the amulet.

SOMEONE was breaking in!

Marissa bolted upright from a dense sleep, sending Harry shooting off the bed with his tail upright. The cat yowled and streaked away into the darkness—toward the sound of the front door closing. That was odd, but Marissa didn't think it through. She was scrabbling over the nightstand to find her phone.

Not there. Not freaking *there*.

She heard a person moving around in the living room without even trying to be quiet. Marissa swallowed thickly as she slid out of bed. Fear was acrid; her mouth tasted like she'd been chewing on tin foil.

Two crimes within hours. Shocking even for a New Yorker.

A light went on in the other room. Marissa dropped down, crouching behind the far side of the bed. She felt around for a weapon, finding a silk scarf, a flimsy chain belt, a Chinese takeout container that had fallen beneath the bed. Maybe there were chopsticks? Why hadn't she obeyed her mother, who'd said that the city was dangerous and Marissa must always sleep with a butcher knife under the mattress?

Aha. A shoe. Her fingers closed on a four-inch heel that could serve as a dagger.

She crept toward the door, shoe in hand. Would a spike heel through an eyeball work as a defense? Only in the movies, but maybe she'd gain time to run out the door.

A thud sounded from the other room, a thud she could have sworn was the sound of feet dropping onto the wood coffee table. She'd heard that thud a hundred times when Jamie came over to watch TV.

But *he* wasn't out there. Unless...

She remembered how they'd kissed on the street and suddenly her lips became plump and tingly. An absurd reaction under the circumstances. Granted, Jamie had a key, but he wouldn't come back—would he?—hoping for...

An early morning booty break-in? Not likely.

Marissa edged out the door, ready to strike even though her confused instincts had taken the fear down a few notches. She knew something wasn't right, but she couldn't tell what.

One small lamp was on, leaving the room filled with dusky shadows. She narrowed her eyes. There was a person on the couch. Bent over. Making shuffling noises.

Going through my stuff. Insulted by the invasion of privacy, Marissa raised the shoe above her head.

Silently she stepped within striking distance. Harry sat on the arm of the sofa with his tail curved around his body, blinking at Marissa as if wondering what had taken her so long.

What the...?

The person on the couch was straightening.

"Freeze!" Changing tactics in an instant, Marissa pressed the sharp heel of the shoe to the intruder's back. "Feel that? That's a gun that'll blow a hole straight through your spine."

3

THE INTRUDER LET OUT a high-pitched yelp. Either his balls had crawled up into his body cavity or he was a woman.

"I said not to move." Marissa dug the heel deeper.

She looked at Harry, who was calmly washing his face with a paw. Simultaneously, Marissa recognized the thief's curly blond head. Her remaining fear drained away.

She dropped the shoe. *"Shandi?"*

The woman corkscrewed around to gape at Marissa, then flopped over on the cushions facedown. "Chh'yah, girl! You scared me to death!"

"I scared you?" Marissa stared down at her former roommate, wondering why she even bothered to be surprised. Shandi Lee was the proverbial bad penny. "I thought I was being burgled."

Shandi rose up on her elbows. "What are you doing here? You said you were going on vacation for a week." She was a pretty girl under the glitz, but beginning to look run down from not taking care of herself. A heavy application of lipstick, mascara and eyeliner had melted and smeared, giving her the look of a sad-eyed clown.

"I'm back early. Man troubles." Marissa crossed her arms. "And you?"

Shandi attempted a chagrined grin, which wasn't very convincing. Her misdeeds were too frequent to be excused as momentary lapses or bad judgment. "You caught me. Since I knew your apartment was empty, I crashed here after Ming kicked me out."

"Ming kicked you out?" *Oh, hell. Another roommate bites the dust.* But Marissa wouldn't be persuaded to provide shelter. Not again. "What did you do this time?"

"Spent my rent on a Fendi purse. Look at it." Shandi pointed at the coffee table, where a pink leather pouch perched atop the stack of fashion magazines, newspapers and junk mail. "It's adorable. *So* worth it."

"The purse is cute," Marissa conceded, adding quickly, "but you can't stay." The roommate before Ming had given Shandi the boot after a raucous New Year's Eve party had resulted in three arrests, two infidelities and one hole punched in the wall. That time, Shandi had bunked on Marissa's couch for a week.

"Aw, c'mon. Don't make me pack up." A pair of Chinese silk pajamas spilled from the open tote bag on the floor. "I'm ready to pass out."

Harry tightroped the back of the couch to press against Marissa's arm. She rubbed the cat's head, weakening. Shandi was like an alley cat—superannoying when yowling at night, but scruffily irresistible when she meowed on the doorstep in the rain. "Okay, you can stay until morning. But you have to find another place tomorrow, okay?"

Shandi flopped again. "I could ask Jamie to lend me a corner."

Marissa stiffened, but she kept her voice casual. "You could."

Shandi's visible eye opened. "If I can get past you."

"I'm not his bodyguard."

Snort. "You're each other's bodyguards. I wish you two would get over yourselves and just do it already."

"Let's not get into that again." Marissa resisted, then couldn't help herself. "We're dogs and cats."

Shandi yawned. "Like that matters when you know he wants to ride you like a mustang."

Marissa didn't reply. The kisses with Jamie remained a bright neon sign at the back of her brain. *¡Dios!* Middle of the night and she was lit up like Broadway. If the mugger hadn't knocked some sense into her earlier, there was no telling how naked they'd be right now.

But she didn't want that…not really. Her resolution was to make no more mistakes. Fooling around with Jamie could be a huge one.

Shandi was smirking into an Ultrasuede sofa pillow. To avoid another bawdy comment, Marissa went to the linen closet and selected a pair of sheets, a blanket and an extra pillow from the jumbled contents. She came back and dropped them on her guest's backside. Not up to Martha Stewart's standards, but then, Marissa hadn't sent out any engraved invitations. "At least take off your shoes."

Shandi lifted her feet up and toed off her Reebok sneakers. The shoes must have weighed five pounds.

They hit the floor like andirons. Better weapons than the sandals, especially when inserted into an open mouth.

Making a note of that, Marissa chirped to Harry and walked back to her bedroom. She softened her tone. "Good night, Shandi." Then couldn't resist. "Please don't get makeup on my pillows."

She left the door open a couple of inches for the cat and crawled into bed. The Habaneros T-shirt she slept in rode up around her waist and she pulled it down, humping her hips a couple of times. The bedsprings squeaked.

In a voice filled with deviltry, Shandi called, "Ride me, big Sheldon," quoting from *When Harry Met Sally*, one of their favorite movie night chick flicks.

"Oh, just shut up," Marissa murmured. She was usually quicker with a comeback, but the skin on her thighs had jumped to her own touch and she was busy thinking how she would have reacted if Jamie had been waiting in bed for her. Gone on a bucking bareback ride? With her platonic pal?

One day ago that notion would have been laughable. Now it wasn't. And what had changed? There was her breakup, but she'd lost boyfriends before and hadn't turned to Jamie except for brotherly comfort. Maybe she was only having an unusually adverse reaction to a bad vacation, complicated by loss of sleep.

She'd be sane by morning.

Instead of wanting Jamie like crazy.

"GIVE ME BACK MY KEY," was the first thing Marissa said the next morning when she passed through the living room to get to the galley kitchen, her eyes crusted into slits. If she didn't take a firm stance from the start, she'd find herself giving in, one night at a time, until she had herself a new roommate.

Her resolve was reinforced when she stumbled over the junk that had been scattered throughout the room. Shandi's worldly possessions—basically a wardrobe, a collection of shoe boxes, one packet of important papers like tax returns and inscribed cocktail napkins and the toolbox that held an oversize makeup kit. Marissa shoved the meager belongings into one big pile. Harry danced ahead, meowing for Fancy Feast.

Shandi muttered something unintelligible and pulled the blanket over her head.

In the kitchen Marissa popped the top of a can of turkey giblets, filled the cat's dish, then got the arabica dark roast coffee beans from the expanding igloo of her freezer. She made the grinder sing like a swarm of killer bees.

Shandi got the hint and staggered to her feet, saying, "Coffee. Need coffee," as she lurched toward the bathroom.

"You're going in the wrong direction." Marissa gave the beans one more good buzz. The rich smell was waking her up too. Soon the past thirty-two hours would make sense.

She was picking at the corners of her eyes, waiting for the coffee to brew and going over all the reasons that Jamie was no good for her as a lover even though he was nothing but good as a friend, when the doorbell rang.

Jamie's eye met hers in the peephole. Marissa wanted to run away back to the bedroom and execute a frantic twenty-second toilette, but Shandi was occupying the bathroom. Acting differently around Jamie would only call attention to how really different Marissa felt since The Kiss.

She scrubbed her hands on her shirt and opened the door, glad she'd pulled on a pair of yoga pants.

A wet nose thrust into her crotch. "Sally!" Jamie tugged at his dog's leash. He offered an easy smile that lessened Marissa's self-consciousness. "Sorry. I was taking the beast out for a run at George's when I heard your coffee grinder."

"I'm still waking up."

His face changed when he heard the shower. "You have company."

Marissa weighed her options. She could tell him Paul had followed her home, they'd made up and that would be that. Except that *wouldn't* be that. Anyone who'd ever seen a romantic comedy starring a Hollywood It girl knew "that" only led to more complications.

Besides, she couldn't lie to Jamie.

Yeah, except about your feelings.

"Shandi showed up after the bars closed, looking for a soft place to land." Marissa leaned in. "Start thinking of your excuses now."

Jamie pulled back. "Uh, the Village chapter of the Angelina Jolie fan club is meeting in my apartment."

"Not bad, but I have lice."

"Then I'm fumigating for cockroaches."

"Spring-cleaning," Marissa said, sure she'd trumped him since she hadn't spring-cleaned since forever.

"Nuclear bomb testing."

She opened her mouth. Nothing came out. Damn. "Come in for coffee," she said, leaving the door open and going back to the kitchen. "But this doesn't mean you win."

"Don't fight over me now." Shandi had come out of the bathroom wrapped in a towel. Her mop of wild curls dripped down her back. "You can split me like my parents did." She gave Jamie's golden retriever a pat. "Daddy, will you buy me a pony?"

He put up his hands, the leash twisting around his wrist. "Sorry. I don't have room for either of you. But if I get a choice, I'd rather muck out after the pony."

"Sheesh. I didn't even ask yet." Shandi dropped onto the couch, pouting. "You two are giving me a complex."

"That'll be the day," Marissa said from the kitchen doorway. Shandi was a creature of airy confidence. She worked off and on as a freelance makeup artist, which meant that she was either flush with funds or flat broke. The state of her finances never bothered her. She lived her life on whims and luck, both good and bad. Unfortunately her morals tended to be as flexible as her address.

"I have a job all next week," Shandi announced. "I'm doing makeup for an episode of 'Law & Order.' And I met a guy last night who's an art director at an ad agency. He loved my book."

"Good. You'll be able to pay for a new room."

"Something really swank. But in the meantime…" Shandi made big eyes at them, looking wan without her makeup.

"No," Marissa and Jamie said in unison. They eyed each other, sending signals. The only way to stand firm was to make a run for it.

Jamie turned to go. "I have to walk the beast before her bladder bursts. Want to—"

"Yes, I'll come." Marissa grabbed her keys out of the straw purse and Shandi's shoes off the floor. She flew out the door, right behind Jamie. "Lock up when you go," she called over her shoulder before slamming the door.

She stabbed her feet into the one-size-too-small shoes. Jamie took her arm. "Let's hurry before she follows us."

"This is so undignified," Marissa said as they hit the street. "We'd better not come across anyone I know. I haven't taken a shower. I'm not even wearing a bra."

His gaze skipped to her boobs. "Um, nice."

"'Um, nice'?" She crossed her arms, then uncrossed them. "Since when?"

"Nice isn't flattering?"

"No, it's— I meant, since when did you notice?"

"I've always noticed when you're not wearing a bra."

"Oh." She counted back in her head and figured that must be about a couple hundred occasions, adding in all their lazy Sundays when she didn't get out of her pajamas till noon. Going without a bra wasn't something she spent a lot of time contemplating. She was small on top and liked it that way.

So did Jamie? *Wow.*

They moved off down the street, heading toward George's, the large-dog run at Washington Square Park.

Her heart was beating like a bongo drum. "How come you never said anything?"

Jamie took a long time answering. "How would you have reacted if I'd mentioned that you look sexy with a little jiggle and perkiness under your shirt? Or if I'd confessed that I steal looks through the gap every time you miss a button?"

Marissa bit the inside of her cheek. "I might have been more careful."

She should feel mortified. Or at least insulted. But the knowledge that he'd been looking at her *that* way, noticing her body and maybe lusting after her hardcore, was not as weird as she'd once have expected. Ever since The Kiss—

No, her feelings had started even before that. Ever since she'd met him at the airport, there was a difference between them.

A difference that made heat crawl through her veins every time she thought about him touching her.

"I'm teasing," Jamie said in a flat voice, his gaze pinned to the dog's flopping ears.

"Yeah?"

"Yeah."

She sensed he was only trying to placate her. "Why don't I believe you?"

He grinned sheepishly, looking a little more like the boy next door who kept her safe instead of off center. "Because when it comes to ogling the naughty bits of naked women, guys will always lie if they think they can get away with it."

"I didn't used to think of you as that kind of guy."

"Then what am I? A eunuch?"

"Of course not! I know you're, well, virile. In fact, you're very attractive. Just not—"

"Just not attractive to you?" They'd slowed. His level, brooding stare was unnerving. But hot. Her cheeks flared. Forget the boy next door. He was giving off heavy-duty, man-in-your-bed vibes.

The old Jamie would have cracked a joke to distract them, but this one wasn't backing down. He said, without a trace of embarrassment, "That's not what your mouth was telling me last night."

She gulped. "I wondered how long it'd take for us to go there." She glanced around at the street, busy with the morning's comings and goings. The dog walkers were out in full force: slender gay men matched with their greyhounds, high-heeled women toting pocket pooches, family guys leashed to a selection of setters and retrievers. "Huh. Not long. We haven't even made it off the block."

Jamie let Sally pull him forward to the corner, the dog's nose quivering as she scented the bursting spring foliage at the park. "You want to pretend it didn't happen?"

"I want us not to change. Not to make one kiss—"

Jamie's new triple-X adult eyes knifed at her.

"Okay, a *few* kisses. Hot ones, even." She took a steadying breath and started again. "Not to make a few hot kisses into some big drama that wrecks our friendship."

"Like I said, you want to forget it happened." Suddenly he sounded sad. Marissa's stomach flipped. "Might as well forget what I said about your breasts, too."

"Whatever. Really, it's no big deal if you snuck a few peeks." She looked down the neck hole of her T-shirt. "Breasts are breasts, unless they're Pamela Anderson's. So what if you've seen mine. I'm not shy."

Jamie made a motion as if he intended to get another look, and she grabbed at the loose fabric, stretching the shirt taut across her front. Her nipples pressed sharp little points against the thin cotton.

The crosswalk light switched. The other pedestrians moved off quickly. Jamie didn't budge an inch. Sally whimpered, tugging at the leash.

"Okay," Marissa said. "You made your point. We can't put the genie back in the bottle. But I'm not ready to deal with this." She made a motion to reach for his hand, then pulled back. "Please, let's go along as usual for a few days. I just got home. I'm wearing Shandi's shoes."

She put a hand up to flip back her hair and her fingers got stuck on a snarl. She *never* went out in such a state of disarray. Even going to the gym required a certain look with a coordinated outfit and her hair in a braided knot. "I'm all out of sorts."

"I understand," Jamie said. Grudgingly, for him. "But I'm not letting this drop for good," he added because he couldn't seem to help it. "You should think about the possibility that our friendship won't be ruined if we become lovers. It might even be enhanced."

"You're such an optimist."

He smiled. "And that's a good thing."

"I'll think about it. But I can't make a decision so fast."

Even though she *always* made decisions fast. "Will you wait? A reprieve is all I need to get my head straight."

Man and dog cocked their heads at her.

"All I need," she repeated, hoping that he couldn't see that her heart was saying something more.

All I need is you.

"That and breakfast." Jamie took her hand and turned Sally loose. The dog bounded into the crosswalk, feathered tail waving like a semaphore. They jogged after her, stretching their legs, and the tension inside Marissa finally let go.

"Do you think she's gone?"

"I don't want to get my hopes up."

Jamie angled his head toward their brownstone. "I hear music. Maroon Five."

"Then she's still there. Damn." Marissa slowly climbed the steps. "I really don't want a roommate again. It's been nice, having the place to myself. My first time completely on my own."

Jamie followed. She'd talked often about her family in Miami, so he knew that she'd grown up poor but ambitious, sharing a tiny bedroom with her sister, dreaming of life in the big city. "I don't want her, either, but if I have to take the bullet, I will."

"No!" Marissa looked startled by her own vehemence. "That is, I don't expect you to sacrifice yourself for my sake. She'll find a place."

He weighed the possibilities. "Are you worried that we'd sleep together?"

"Who? Us?"

He could only hope. "Me and Shandi."

Cool now, Marissa raised an eyebrow. "Would you?"

"Hell, no." When he ran into Shandi these days, he couldn't remember why he'd ever been involved with her. Thinking about it, he saw that she'd dazzled him with her freewheeling zest, somewhat like Marissa. Shandi Lee was an experience. Three years ago, he'd still been new to the city lifestyle, recently removed from a comfortable suburban home. He had commuted to college, then put in a short stint at a small-town paper before realizing that he'd become *too* settled.

But he'd progressed since his first days in the city. He'd become a lot smarter about what kind of woman he wanted in his life.

"You liked her once," Marissa ventured.

"Uh, I still do." *Even if he didn't entirely trust her.*

"You liked her in a romantic way."

"Well, you were with…what was his name?"

"Ivan. He's a cancer researcher now, you know, at Sloan Kettering."

"Impressive." Marissa's men usually had careers of importance or wealth. Jamie would never accomplish either with his average-paying job at the *Village Observer*. His big attempt at ambition was ghost-writing a biography with a rock legend, a project that had hit a major pothole when he'd realized the man was functionally illiterate.

Marissa had unlocked the front door. She turned her eyes on him. They were clear and unblinking, framed in a fringe of dark lashes. "No, I don't want Ivan back."

"And I don't want Shandi."

"Then we're agreed. We'll *all* be just friends."

Little did she know. After Sally's sojourn in the park, they'd gone to Blue Dog's Café, a popular coffeehouse with huge breakfasts and free doggie biscuits at the counter. Marissa had excused herself and come back with her hair finger-combed and the baggy T-shirt knotted above her belly button. Without makeup, her face glowed. Her bare lips were full and soft. He'd found it tough to pull his gaze away, although her natural beauty was daunting. She could emerge from a ragbag and still pull herself together, while he counted himself dapper if he remembered to put on an unwrinkled shirt.

Over a tofu and spinach scramble, she'd continued with her insistence that this wasn't the right time to start up anything between them. He'd agreed against every instinct, silently planning to bide his time until she adjusted to the idea.

The situation might have seemed hopeless. Except that he'd been struck by the way she'd avoided touching him. At first. And proof that she was as aware of him as he was of her.

The dog, who'd been sniffing at a concrete urn holding only the stiff brown stalks of last year's planting, suddenly gave one short sharp bark. She shot to the end of the leash. The jolt almost jerked Jamie off his feet. "Sally! Quiet."

Marissa stood at his shoulder. "What is it?"

"There must have been a cat." He looked across the

street. A woman pushed a stroller. A man in an ill-fitting business suit leaned against a mailbox, head lowered while he lit a cigarette. Sally growled low in her throat.

"I'm jumpy since the mugging attempt," said Marissa. "I even thought Shandi was a burglar."

"I'll keep an eye out." Jamie squeezed her hand.

The gesture was innocent, then not. They realized their proximity at the same moment. His gaze caught on her lips. She dented the lower one with her teeth. They leaned even closer, inches away, holding their breath—

"Hey, hey, hey! What's going on here?" called a voice from above. Shandi hung out of the third-floor window. "Break it up, you guys."

Marissa pulled away, her cheeks almost as pink as her lips.

"Would you mind answering your cell?" Cavalierly, Shandi tossed the phone out the window. "It's driving me up the wall, ringing every ten minutes."

Jamie made a lunge and caught the phone. He handed it to Marissa. "I thought it was switched off," she said when the shrill ringer went off.

Shandi grimaced. "Yeah, well, I had to make a few calls and my minutes are running short. Quid pro quo— you stole my shoes."

"Great." Marissa flipped the phone open and said a wary "Hello?"

A deep voice immediately began fast talking on the other end of the connection. Jamie knew by the way her face sobered that the caller was Paul Beckwith. What he couldn't tell was whether she'd wanted to hear from him.

4

"I'M HANGING UP now, Paul."

He continued as if Marissa hadn't spoken, essentially pleading for her forgiveness even though he talked around any actual admission of wrongdoing. Why hadn't she ever noticed that he was as slick as a politician—or the stereotypical smarmy lawyer? Especially when cornered.

She broke in. "All I hear is yammering that doesn't mean a thing to me. I'm hanging up."

"First say that you're not angry with me."

"Fine. I was angry, but I'm not anymore. Okay?"

"You still sound angry." Paul inhaled as if he were going to relaunch, but maybe he'd finally run out of words because he actually waited for her reply.

Marissa sat on her bed cross-legged. Shandi was in the kitchen, making pancakes in animal shapes. With a nonchalant shrug, Jamie had signaled to Marissa that he was going upstairs to his place. She'd been relieved that he didn't feel the need to stick around and coach her on her responses to Paul—while listening in—but another part of her kind of wished that he was the type of guy who fought for what he wanted.

"Marissa?" Paul said. "Are you still there?"

"I'm here. I don't know why."

"You *are* angry."

"I'm disgusted, yes. I know where you went, the night I left."

A pause stretched, then Paul asked, "How do you know?"

"I saw you from the hotel balcony. Through my camera."

More of the elastic pause. "Your camera?"

"I was taking pictures."

"Pictures?" Paul's voice was strangled. "Of me?"

"Why would I want a picture of my cheating boy-friend?"

"So you didn't—" He exhaled. "About that. It's not what you think."

"Was she good, the blonde?"

"Marissa. Sweetheart. You've got it all wrong. I didn't cheat on you."

"Your hands were all over her. She stuck her tongue in your ear."

"You saw a lot. Did you see…"

His Hugo Boss-tailored erection? Yes, indeed.

"Did you see my client, too?"

Marissa blinked. Paul was worried about the client instead of defending himself? He must be *really* guilty. Of something. "I had a glimpse."

"Listen, Marissa. This is important. I can't get back to the city yet. I have more to accomplish here—"

"I'm sure. Lots of island beach bunnies to catch."

Paul got all stuffy. "Regardless of what you think you saw, this is business. Company business. It would be beneficial to your career at Howard, Coffman if you set aside your pride and just kept your mouth shut."

Marissa was ready to feel insulted by his assumption that she would act like a wronged "wife" in the office, until she realized that this wasn't about their relationship. Paul was trying to secure her silence. "What *were* you doing, holding a meeting in a parking lot?"

"Nothing you need to be concerned with."

"But *you* are. Concerned."

"I'm concerned for how you're feeling," Paul said in his slippery way.

"Uh-huh." She pulled the phone away and rolled her eyes at it. "I'm *really* hanging up now. Rest assured, I have no intentions of telling tales at the office."

"You're not due back yet. They don't expect you until Monday."

"True." Let him think she wasn't going in. "If you're finished with your top-secret meetings by then, you can be there in person to be sure I don't besmirch your sterling reputation."

"You always were a smart cookie, Marissa."

Cookie? She didn't crumble that easily.

"Oh, absolutely." She couldn't resist making a dig so he'd have something to worry about. "I won't even show around the photos of our—your—romantic rendezvous. Ta-ta!" Marissa laughed gaily and clicked off on Paul's stuttering response.

Shandi stood in the doorway with a pancake on a

spatula. Her expression was almost apprehensive. "I made a turtle," she said awkwardly, "and there's burned sausage, too." Behind her, the air near the ceiling was layered with smoke. "What did Paul want?"

"I'm not quite sure."

"Sounded like he was trying to make up with you."

"No, actually, I wasn't his top priority. At least not the me he sees outside of the office." Marissa frowned, absorbed in replaying the conversation. Paul was worried about what she'd seen—and who she'd tell. He knew she had the ear of Thomas Howard, a senior partner. His blather about making up with her was just a smokescreen.

"Do you want the turtle?" Shandi asked, lifting the pancake toward Marissa.

"Thanks, but no. I ate breakfast with Jamie."

"You two…" Shandi put a finger on the pancake to hold it in place as she turned to go. "Three's a crowd. I'll pack up and be out of here as soon as I can."

"Take your time," Marissa said. She was distracted, trying to remember where she'd dumped her luggage. In the closet? No, under the bed. She dove forward on her stomach and reached for the handle. The suitcase was caught on something and she yanked it free.

The bag was upside down with the zipper half undone. Her stuff spilled from the gap. Damp swimsuits. Ew. At least she'd wrapped them in a towel.

A hotel towel. Bad girl.

She dropped the suits on the carpet and pawed through the other tumbled garments, setting aside two pairs of shoes before tipping over the suitcase to form a dirty laundry pile. After a cursory check of the outside pocket, the bag went back under the bed empty. What a crummy trip it had been. No souvenirs, not even a postcard.

Shandi had returned to the doorway, licking syrup off a fork. "What are you looking for?"

"My reason."

"Reason for what?"

"Not that kind of reason." Marissa sat up and ripped off her sleep shirt. Gross. She'd actually worn it outside. She might be a slob in the housekeeping department, but she liked to look good. Maybe she'd become too comfortable around Jamie.

No longer a problem.

She sighed. "I've lost my head. And damn if my libido isn't working overtime."

Shandi grinned. "Oh, so you meant a reason to jump Jamie's tush?"

"That would be entirely unreasonable," Marissa muttered from inside her closet. She'd left her robe hanging on a hook on the back of the door. It wasn't there. Or on the floor, among the tangle of strappy sandals and unmatched socks. "Did you use my robe?"

"I might have." Shandi made an *oops* face beneath her halo of tumbled curls. "Someone came to the door when I was still in a towel. Must have been one of your old boyfriends, because he was surprised when I answered."

"None of my old boyfriends would expect me to be at home on a Wednesday." Marissa found a silk kimono and slipped that on. She wiggled out of the yoga pants. "I hope you didn't let him in."

"Do I look like I'm fresh off the farm?" Shandi asked. She was from Nebraska, where her single mom was a Mary Kay consultant. Shandi liked to say that foundation ran in her veins.

"No, but knowing you, you'd have thought his dimples were cute and five minutes later he's your best bud and you're feeding him macadamia-nut cookies from my secret stash."

Shandi considered. "He wasn't that type of guy. In fact, I just realized that he wasn't your type of guy at all, even though he wore a suit."

"I'm done with 'my type,'" Marissa said from the bathroom. The pipes clanked inside the wall when she turned on the taps. C'mon, baby, she pleaded with the recalcitrant plumbing. She shed the robe, always the optimist. The showers at her gym were hot and hard enough to satisfy any single girl, but she couldn't go another minute without washing away the stink of the bad trip with Paul. Maybe any lingering inclinations for her old type of guy would also go down the drain.

"One question," Shandi said, practically following her into the tub.

"Go ahead." Marissa stuck her head under the thin, lukewarm spray. "But if you're going to ask me about Jamie, don't bother because I have no idea." *No idea, that is, except for the one where he's a Bedouin raider and I'm a captive princess, lying naked in a desert tent when he comes to me with his body all hot and hard and whooo, boy, talk about libidos in overdrive.*

Shandi stuck her head past the shower curtain. "All I want to know is where you hide the cookies."

"WHAT'RE YOU WORKING ON?" asked Skip Sisman, the metro reporter who'd never met a pastry he didn't like. "A revival of *Sound of Music*?" He guffawed around a bite of something crusty and oozing. Singing nuns were high humor in Skip's world.

Jamie closed his laptop and slid it out of pastry flake range. Early that morning, he'd e-mailed a book review to the copy desk. But after leaving Marissa on the phone with Paul, he'd been too antsy to sit at home. He'd come into work to pick up his mail and whip out a few hundred filler words on the new CD from Overdog, four teenagers from the lower East Side who were too cool to realize they were basically just another boy band. His comments were kind. He'd been there with his own band, back when he didn't yet know that he was hopelessly uncool.

Jamie tilted back in his chair and gave Sisman the fish eye. "What are *you* working on? The fascinating ins and outs of the fifth day of the garbage strike?"

"Following up on the theft at Stanhope's. There was a rumor the thief was caught trying to leave the country with the goods, but my inside source says that was bull. Nobody's in custody."

Sisman was always citing his inside source, as if everyone at the paper didn't know the big contact was his aunt Dena, who worked the switchboard at One Police Plaza and was the queen bee of information gathering. Her drones were in every precinct in the city, from property clerks to the receptionist at the coroner's office. As sources went, Aunt Dena was a valuable one. Sisman rarely left his desk, except for bakery runs.

"I thought there'd been a break in the case." One of the pieces had supposedly shown up in a Queens pawn shop. Sisman had made a big deal of his "investigation."

"That went nowhere," the reporter admitted. "But I hear the people at Stanhope's are screaming to the right people. Ergo, the mayor's office is tightening the screws on the police force." Sisman sat on the corner of Jamie's desk, getting cozy. A ring of fat lapped his belt like an overinflated inner tube.

Jamie reminded himself to cut out the midday doughnuts if he wanted to keep up with Marissa. "Then you'd better get on the big story."

Sisman licked filling out of the pastry. "You're the arts guy."

"I am." The staff at the *Village Observer* was small, so most of them doubled up on responsibilities. Jamie's duties included every opening from gallery to letter.

"Then you'd know about the White Star."

The ancient ivory amulet known as the White Star had been one of the pieces stolen from Stanhope's. Jamie shook his head. "Never heard of it until the heist."

"Yeah, that's the rub. Here's this supposedly rare and valuable *tschotske* and nobody knows about it, not even you art-loving types. How come?"

"It's been in private collections."

"Interesting." Sisman popped the last bite into his mouth.

"Not really." Jamie opened his laptop, then closed it again while Sisman brushed off his sweater. "What are you after, Skip?"

"The Wart Hog wants a sidebar on the amulet. You could research it."

"You kidding me? I'm not doing your work."

"Okay, so you write the piece and get a byline."

"Go talk to Alice in Features."

"I tried. She sent me to you."

To the moon, Alice. "Then go bug someone else. Anyone else. The intern or the bike messenger. I have enough on my plate."

Sisman poked the thick ARC—advance reader copy—that had come in yesterday's mail from one of the big publishers, along with a packet of promo materials and a plea for column inches. "The Savvy Woman's Guide To Breast Feeding. Yeah, that sounds fascinating."

The man had a point. "But there are breasts involved. Which makes it far more fascinating than some dusty old relic."

Sisman heaved himself off the desk. "Any pictures in there?"

Jamie laughed. "Changing your tune, huh?" Maybe he could turn the tables and con Sisman into writing the review or taking over his tickets to the Streetcorner Player's experimental version of *Guys and Dolls*.

"So you won't help?" Sisman pushed.

"Nope. Unless you're willing to make a deal."

"Not if it involves breast pumps."

After Sisman had lumbered away, Jamie reached for the phone, feeling like he was fifteen again and calling for his first date.

"Hey, Jamie," Marissa said after the second ring.

"You're picking up again."

"Only when I recognize the number."

"Paul's still in the Caribbean?" *Subtext: he's not racing home to win back your heart?*

"As far as I know. Let's not waste our time talking about him, okay?"

He heard her panting and for a moment thought she was overwrought until the rhythmic whirring sound penetrated his brain. "You're at the gym."

"Yep."

"Got plans after that?"

Whirr-whirr-whirr. "Nope, except for a few errands. Since I'm officially on vaycay, I gave myself a day all to myself. Tomorrow's soon enough to go back to work."

Technically she didn't have to return until Monday, but he didn't bother to point that out. The law firm was her surrogate family, workaholic style. "Want to have lunch?"

"We already had breakfast."

"A late lunch."

The whirring picked up its pace. "No, I'll just get a smoothie at the juice bar."

Jamie swallowed. "Dinner?"

"I think—" she panted "—I'm going out with Shandi."

"Oh. She's still at your place?"

"For one more night."

"Sure, sure."

Marissa laughed. "She caught me at a moment of weakness."

"You have those?"

"You of all people know that I do."

"Yeah, but you bounce back so fast, I wonder if you purposely choose men you don't truly care about so the split won't slow you down."

"My moments of weakness don't *all* involve men." *Whirr. Whirr. Whirr.* She was thinking faster than she was pedaling. "Well, maybe they do." More pedaling. "So you think I'm calculating?"

"Of course not."

"But I am without mercy."

"That depends."

"Fierce? You've got to give me fierce."

"Hell, yeah."

"Cold-blooded?"

"Not necessarily. You run hot and cold."

She stopped pedaling. He heard only the more distant whirring of the other bicyclists, underlaid with the clank of weights and peppy aerobic music. He waited, drumming his fingers on the desktop.

Finally she let out a big breath. "Hot and cold, huh? Then how come *you* make me feel warm?"

He leaned forward in his chair, took a quick glance around the newsroom, then dropped his head so low it almost hit the desk. His voice came out like gravel. "When do I make you feel warm?"

"When your voice gets like that."

He couldn't reply.

She was whispering. "When I know you're keeping your feelings inside so you don't spook me."

"Fierce women spook?"

"Sometimes."

"I don't want you spooked."

"But you do want me."

"Yes."

There was another long silence.

"You don't feel the same way," he said, pinching the bridge of his nose.

"I don't know. I mean, I do, but I don't. Shandi says that the only way for me to get over Paul is to get under someone else. You know how she is. So that's why we're going out—manhunting. I didn't tell her…"

"That *I'm* the man." He was surprised by the confidence that poured into the statement. Given one small opening, his suppressed desire would erupt like a volcano.

Marissa had better be sure.

So had he, after hesitating for three long years.

"Shandi's always suspected it, way before I did. I thought she was loco, at first, going on about how you had it bad for me."

He felt his face redden. "No kidding? You never said. How long has this been common knowledge?"

"Oh, you know. Girl talk. But it wasn't knowledge. Only supposition."

He'd thought she told him everything, including the girl talk. It was good to hear he'd been wrong.

"So how about an early dinner?" he suggested. "You know Shandi won't be ready to go out for hours."

Marissa answered quickly. "No. We can't go out romantically when we've decided to stay friends."

Stabbed in the gut. "I didn't mention romance."

"It's in your voice."

And she wasn't having any.

"I'm sorry," she said. "I just can't."

"Then I'll see you around."

"Don't go away mad."

"Just go away?"

"For now, yes." Her voice was gentle.

He hung up, feeling almost as crummy as he had when Carly Bibb, tenth-grade siren, had turned down his invitation to see *Wayne's World.* He'd hung up the phone four times before he'd worked up the courage to say hello.

An unsettling similarity.

Was it only the adrenaline that had rushed him into kissing Marissa?

5

As soon as darkness had fallen, Jean Allard scaled the fire escape, a rusty structure that clung to the backside of the five-story brownstone via a zigzag pattern of ancient bolts. The steps would rattle menacingly under the weight and motion of any normal person. *La Souri Noire*, however, passed without a sound. He was accustomed to squeezing in and out of much tighter spots.

At the third floor, he moved nearer the window, where a shadow was thrown against the blocks of stone. He waited there, uneasy.

It was too early—lights were on in many of the windows of the surrounding buildings. He ran a great risk of being spotted.

Allard's employer had not been pleased with the delay in the delivery of the White Star, but he had understood what was necessary. Now that the officials were stepping up their search for the thief, he must move even more carefully. Haste would be disastrous.

As would seeing the White Star slip away between his fingers, Allard thought as he leaned away from the wall. He had to be positive that the girl hadn't discovered the amulet in her luggage.

Beyond the lace curtain, a small lamp glowed within Marissa Suarez's bedroom. She was home. The roommate, also. He'd already known that, having watched their front door from the street most of the day.

The roommate had been an unpleasant surprise. In his preliminary survey, he'd checked the label on the mailbox for Apt 3C, even picked its lock to go through the contents. All of the mail had been under one name: Marissa Suarez. And yet the girl with the curly hair had been home when he'd expected the apartment to be empty.

Another small complication, but no matter. He knew where to focus.

Allard's eyes narrowed. Marissa was in bed, already sleeping.

He admired her bare legs, the curve of her hip. She wore a pair of bikini panties and a small T-shirt that rose above her ribs. Jet hair spilled across the pillow.

He almost smiled at the sight, before remembering that he wasn't here to admire the girl's beauty.

Was the amulet safe? Allard's eyes searched.

At first he believed that the suitcase had been moved. A blade of apprehension sliced through his calm. Beads of perspiration popped up along his hairline, above his lip. But he didn't flinch, except for the near-frantic flicker of his eyes.

Ah, yes! There was the bag—still under the bed, but pushed farther back, almost hidden by the ruffled bedskirt.

Allard was not comforted. Since the suitcase had been moved, there was a good chance she'd unpacked.

Had she found the amulet?

He told himself that was unlikely. He had followed her, first to breakfast, then later while she went on a few errands and to the gym. There had been no sign of the sort of fuss the discovery of the White Star would create.

And yet…he couldn't know for certain. He might have to risk a recovery attempt sooner than was safe.

On the bed, Marissa murmured in her sleep. She became restless, a tremor moving through her lithe body like a wave on the shore. She flipped from her side to her back, frozen for an instant before she relaxed with a sigh.

Dreaming. Allard watched, momentarily forgetting his concern for the amulet. Her hand slipped across her thighs, the fingers moving, caressing. She writhed. She moaned, opening her lips with the tip of her tongue.

His detached interest stirred into arousal. Perhaps he'd been too quick to dismiss the option of introducing himself to Marissa and gaining access to her bedroom through her delectable body.

He leaned closer, intent on seeing more.

The cat sprang into the window with a loud *miaow*, its eyes reflecting an eerie sheen split by narrow black pupils.

Allard jerked back from the glass. The creature bared its small, sharp teeth and hissed.

Marissa had awakened. "Harry?" Allard heard her say, but then he was gone, gliding down the rusty steps, swinging over the railing and landing in a crouch before he scurried off through the narrow, dank span between buildings.

IT WAS half past two in the morning when Marissa returned alone to the apartment after the girls' night out. She was tired even though she'd napped earlier to combat jet lag. Shandi had taken off with a guy, ostensibly to try a hip new club. Marissa wasn't expecting her to return, which was just as well. After having the nap interrupted by a sexy dream that had expanded on her Bedouin fantasy—starring Jamie!—and then Harry's restlessness, she could use a good night's sleep.

She needed a clear head to deal with the Jamie decision.

Oh, Jamie. She'd been so blind about him and their physical attraction. But the thought of losing her best friend over a brief fling filled her with dread.

Her key didn't work. She put her shoulder to the door and jiggled the key in the lock until it turned, noticing the scratches as the door swung open.

The apartment was black. Too black.

Her hackles rose. She imagined she heard breathing, then realized it was her own.

The sconce near the front door should have been on. Perhaps the bulb had burned out.

At first she couldn't put her finger on what else was wrong. Then she knew. She should have been able to see the red digital clock on the DVD player even when all the other lights were off.

Maybe the electricity was out?

The light switch was near the door, but Marissa was frozen. The scratches on the lock…

She'd been burgled.

"Harry?" she quailed. That broke her paralysis. The standard for break-ins was to leave the apartment immediately in case the burglar was still inside, but she wasn't fleeing without her cat.

She hit the switch and the lights came on. The apartment was beyond its usual state of upheaval. Every item on the shelves on the opposite wall, including the TV and DVD player, had been overturned. Drawers were open, couch cushions thrown around. The coatrack was tipped over, with the bags that usually hung from it scattered all around, every one of them yawning open. Their contents littered the floor—forgotten jewelry, coins, receipts, tubes of lipstick.

"Harry?" Marissa called, pushing the door open wider. It seemed to be blocked by something bulky. She took one cautious step inside. "C'mere, kitty, kitty." He was probably hiding under the bed.

Two things happened at once. The cat streaked out of the bedroom, his tail the size of a bottle brush. And the door that Marissa had pushed against came back at her—hard. She staggered.

A man leaped out. He was dressed in black, with his face covered by a ski mask. She saw eyes rimmed in white, a mouth pulled into a snarl.

And then his hand was locked around her wrist and he yanked her into the apartment. The door slammed behind her.

Marissa screamed.

The intruder jerked her arm behind her back, bending it to the breaking point. A gloved hand slapped over her mouth. "Make another sound and I'll snap your arm in half," he rasped into her ear.

He'd pulled her against his thick, muscled body. She caught the scent of liquor and rotting teeth and jerked her head aside.

Hard fingertips dug into her cheek, holding her still. "Where is it?"

Her heart knotted in her throat. She shook her head.

He breathed heavily against her neck, making the small dangling stones of her earring sway. "Tell me where it is and I'll let you go."

His hand was still clamped over her mouth. He didn't get that she couldn't talk until she made a choking sound in her throat.

He dropped his hand to her neck. "Don't scream, bitch," he warned as his grip on her wrist tightened. He sharpened the angle of her arm. A stinging pain shot through it, lodging a burning coal in her shoulder.

Her eyes darted over the mess, wishing for a weapon or a clue. What had he been looking for? Other than a few pricey designer items from her wardrobe and the gold crucifix her parents had given her for confirmation, she had nothing of great value.

"But I don't know what you want," she said in a hoarse whisper.

"You brought it home."

"What? When?"

His fetid breath made her face contort. "From the airport," he said. "We know what you did."

Her voice rose to a soprano pitch. "I brought noth—"

The hand covered her mouth again, smothering the denial.

She whimpered. A pitiful sound, but she wasn't as tough as she'd thought.

Jamie, she called silently. *Please help.* Maybe if she could get free, tip over a chair or slam a door. But he was two floors above. He'd never hear.

"My luggage," she blurted. "The bag, there." She nodded toward the big straw purse, but obviously he'd already been through it. Her passport had been tossed aside, the fashion magazine lay splayed with torn pages. The camera was in pieces, apparently smashed against the floor.

"Where's the rest of it?"

"In the b-bedroom." Marissa's lungs seized. *¡Dios mio!* she didn't want to go in there with him!

He dragged her toward the dark end of the apartment. Marissa pretended to stumble over the coatrack and he loosened his hold, reaching past her to push the tall column aside.

With a stab of pain, she wrenched free. Her captor let out a roar as she leaped like a gazelle across the coatrack. He grabbed at her, but she was too quick. He got only a fistful of long black hair.

She ran into the bedroom, slammed and locked the door, knowing it wouldn't hold even before his body crashed against the barrier. She leaned her weight against it. *Bang.* He hit it again. The door bulged inward. She wished she'd eaten more pancakes and Twinkies.

Bang. The entire wall reverberated. Surely someone would hear and call 9-1-1.

She scanned the top of the nearby chest of drawers for a weapon, then realized she still had her bag. The lightweight evening purse was strung across her chest on a narrow strap, but it had become twisted so the beaded bag was at her back. She didn't dare let up her stance to wrestle out the cell phone.

Bang. The intruder cursed. "Let me in and you won't get hurt."

Really. Did anyone ever believe that cliché?

"Stand back," she called, giving the doorknob a jiggle. He'd have to be an idiot to believe she'd let him in, but she needed only a few seconds. Risking that he was that dumb, she stepped away from the door and with all her might shoved the bureau a few feet over. That wouldn't hold him, either. But she might have time to crawl out the window.

The knob rattled. "Bitch!" *Bang.*

She crossed the room in a flash. She grabbed at her purse, but the window was stuck and she had to use both hands to wrench it open. Praying that Harry had hidden himself well, she scrambled out onto the fire escape. One of her shoes fell off, bounced off the open metal stairs and dropped thirty feet to the cracked pavement.

She glanced down. Her stomach lurched. Incredibly, a second man in black stood at the foot of the fire escape, looking up at her. His glare was lethal. She had the strange sense that she'd seen him before.

They stared at each other, paralyzed. Only for a moment before Marissa's senses returned. She became aware of the aches in her body, the cool air against her hot skin, the rough bite of the metal platform on her bare sole.

There was a great crash from inside the bedroom as the bureau tipped over. She jerked out of her trance to let out a gut-busting scream.

She began climbing. "Jamie! Help!" The staircase structure shook alarmingly as the burglar followed her onto it.

Gasping desperately, she climbed faster. "Oh, please, someone help." Her foot skidded. Damn high heels. She kicked away the other shoe, hoping it would knock her pursuer in the head.

She was so exposed. If either of the men had a gun…
Don't think. Climb!

Above her, a light blinked on behind the curtains. It grew brighter, a precious salvation pouring out of the building as the curtains were drawn aside. The window opened with a screech of the sash. Silhouetted head and shoulders appeared.

"Oh, God, Jamie. Call 9-1-1!"

He didn't. He was out of the window in a shot, dangling himself by one arm through the stairwell to grab hold of her hand and pull her up. She seemed to fly the last few feet.

With a sob, she threw herself into Jamie's arms. He was rock-steady, warm with sleep. "Go, go, go," she urged. "They're coming!"

He looked down. "Who?"

"The burglars." She peered past the railing. The fire escape was empty. "I swear, they were—"

"Get inside," Jamie said, boosting her through his open window.

"You don't believe me."

"Of course I believe you." He climbed in after her and shut the window, then swung an iron safety gate back in place with a heavy *clink*—the type of device he'd asked to install at her place. She'd put him off.

Her teeth chattered as she opened the purse. "He was in my apartment when I got home. I climbed out the window." She gave the cell phone to Jamie. "You call."

Jamie kept his arm around her while he made the emergency call. Then he walked her to the bed—a pull-out sofa—and sat her down on it. He wrapped her in a blanket, telling her that the police would arrive soon. Not always the case, but they were top priority as a crime in progress. "What happened to your shoes?"

"I don't re—" Her brain wasn't working right, all stutters and stops. She shook her head, remembering the clatter of the falling shoe, the face staring up at her. "They came off."

He tucked her cold feet in beneath the blanket. "I'm going to leave you here for a minute while I go downstairs to check this out."

She clutched him, worried for the cat but more worried for Jamie. "Don't do that. They might be there."

"I doubt it."

"But they *could* be. He was looking for something."

"The burglar? What?"

"I'm not sure." She burrowed deeper into the blanket, her mind settling enough to thank God for keeping her safe before it turned to the confusion of the attempted burglary. "Something I brought home from the Caymans."

"Hmm." Jamie paced out his front door and listened for sounds from the stairwell. His hair was tousled and he wore only a pair of boxers. Muscles flexed, tight with tension. The patch on his chest was thicker and darker than she remembered. He seemed macho, even…lusty.

Marissa shivered. Maybe it was the danger, giving her a new perspective. Climbing the stairs, desperate with fear, she'd pinned all her hopes on reaching Jamie. She'd known she could count on him to be there for her.

He stayed out in the hallway, leaning over the stair rail. "It's okay, babe."

She tried to figure out what the intruder might have been looking for, which only made her remember the horror of being captured in the thief's arms. She pushed that out of her mind.

Stay cool, remember to breathe. Every time she inhaled, she felt better. The soft woolen blanket smelled like Jamie. The comfort of that calmed her, sliding through her like warm butter.

When he came back into the room, she opened her arms to him. "Hold me."

He climbed up beside her. "Cold?"

"No, I want—" Her voice caught. What she wanted was a surprise. Her blood hummed with desire. "Just hold me," she begged, aware that her need was entwined with the adrenaline from her escape and a kind of achiness that was also tinged with homesickness. She was restless, ardent, aflame. She wanted to get close to Jamie—body-on-body close. Skin-to-skin. Tongue-in-mouth.

A reaction to the danger…or a decision on their relationship?

Did it matter?

"Kiss me," she said. "Make me warm."

Jamie was nonplused, but the gleam in his eyes told her that he was tempted. "The police will be here—"

"Then hurry." Giving him no choice, she wound her arms around his neck and pulled him down onto the bed. On top of her. His hands went to her breasts. No mistake. One hand on each breast, his fingers tightening on her flesh, kneading it, massaging the surface sensation into a deeper passion that made her tremble and moan and open her mouth against his jaw.

His stubble scraped her lips. But then his sleek mouth and supple tongue took over and she was lost in the hot suction that pulled pleasure through the center of her body in an electric current. Her hair raised at the roots. She couldn't stop moving, hips squirming, legs working.

Her hands traveled over Jamie's bare back. His skin flinched at her touch. Muscles jumped, tensed. He couldn't hold back a groan.

She felt the solidness of him beneath her palms. Gratitude spread through her. He was so alive, so present, so *real*. There was no pretension about Jamie. She was damn lucky to have him.

So go ahead and have him.

She reached between them, trying to lift her own top.

"Wait," Jamie said against her mouth.

"Wait? *Wait?* You're not supposed to say *wait* when I'm taking off my—"

"Allow me." He chuckled at her impatience and slid his hands under her shirt.

She sighed with her entire body and let the assertiveness go. For what felt like the first time in her life, she didn't have to be in charge.

How astonishing that the man who could take over was *Jamie.*

Maybe she should have seen that coming. Friends first. She'd learned to trust him all the way.

It might have been awkward to have her good friend Jamie kneeling between her legs with his hands under her shirt and his thigh pressed where she was hot and swollen and tingling with arousal. It might have been weird to see the bright spark of lust in his eyes.

But somehow it just seemed right.

Anticipation caught in her throat when he rose up enough to straighten his arms, his intense concentration targeted on her breasts. He strummed her nipples. She gasped and arched her back, inhaling again when the motion rubbed her sex against his leg. Her short skirt was flipped up across her hipbone. Underneath she wore a pair of bikini panties. One thin layer of cotton, dampened and sticking to her skin, begging to be torn away.

Jamie wasn't in a hurry. Slowly he dragged up the hem of her skimpy little top, a silk shell trimmed in lace that scratched her rib cage and caught on the tips of her nipples. He hesitated there, looking at her, then deliberately lifted his hands away.

"You're beautiful," he said.

She felt precious, valued. *Loved.*

"And we're stopping." He tugged the lace hem down.

Talk about your buckets of cold water. She struggled up to her elbows. "We're stopping?"

"The police are on the way. And…"

She pressed her thigh between his legs. He was hot and hard.

"I'm not rushing," he said through gritted teeth as he moved her thigh away and swung his legs off her. "When we do this, it's going to be with forethought and all the time in the world."

"Due deliberation?" She dropped flat on the bed and stared at the ceiling, wondering if she should count to ten and find that her sizzling need had gone away. Maybe after a thousand.

"That's nice and all," she said, watching his face with her head lifted an inch off the pillow, "but who says we can only do it once?"

He lifted a wicked eyebrow. "Not me."

The promise of that thrilled her. She closed her eyes and pictured him doing her with all due deliberation, taking his time as he licked and sucked every inch of her before finally thrusting inside, deep inside, so very deep inside.

In her stomach, butterflies took flight. She gave him a wry look to counteract the fluttering. "This is so strange, to be having this conversation with you."

"Ugh. That's what I wanted to avoid." He swooped over her, bringing his face so close that her vision blurred. Her eyes shut again and she concentrated on his mouth, moving against her lips in a talking kiss. "Don't think."

The sudden, stark desire had made her voice husky. "There's a way to stop me from thinking."

"Ah, but that won't last forever."

"Oh?" Why was she disappointed? She wasn't prepared to think in terms of forever, or so she'd told herself each time another guy disappointed her.

"I…meant…sex," Jamie said, planting wet, plucking kisses between every word. "We can't do it *all* the time." He pulled the blanket around them like a hood. She was warm—very warm. And still very aroused. "In between, you'll think of reasons to screw up the relationship."

Her smile curved into his next kiss. "Not if the other kind of screwing's any good."

He touched his lips to her forehead. "No pressure, hmm?"

She was surprised by the amused confidence of his tone. When had Jamie become so sure of himself? She'd always been the lead dog in their friendship, the one who came up with plans and issued invitations, from the very first day when she'd arrived at his hole-in-the-wall apartment in the East Village with an ice pack for his nose and box seat tickets to the Yankees. Back then, his approach with women had been boyishly self-effacing, even a little bit bashful. Since he also happened to be good-looking, plenty of women had found him adorably date-worthy.

They were such close friends, Marissa hadn't really noticed that he'd changed. But he had.

He's a man now, not a boy.

"You're pretty sure of yourself." She took his hand, directing it toward her breast.

His fingers folded up. He wouldn't touch her there. "And you're a temptress. Don't get me started."

"Such resolve." She flung out her arms, giving up on persuasion.

"That's easy when I'm committed," he said, kissing her once more as a siren blasted out on the street.

She didn't get to ask him what that meant, but merely the word made her heart go *thump*.

Not necessarily in a good way.

6

"SO THE ENTIRE PLACE was tossed," said one of New York's finest at the door to the bedroom.

"Let me see." Cradling Harry to her chest, Marissa squeezed past the police officer and the bureau that had been upended when the intruder forced the door. She was wearing an old Lollapalooza sweatshirt of Jamie's. Barely an inch of skirt showed beneath it, making her legs look even longer and definitely more naked.

Jamie had seen the pair of officers checking her out. Butch and beefy in their uniforms, they'd puffed up their chests and gained much enthusiasm for the call when Marissa had met them in the hallway. She was so sexy and tousled even the man in the moon would have noticed if given a peek.

A small jewelry box had been knocked off the dresser. She let Harry go and he sprang onto the bed with a yowl, still upset that he'd been deserted despite Marissa's reassuring hugs. She dusted off her hands and poked through the scattered jewelry, then moved around the room, checking for missing or misplaced items.

"Actually, I don't think he was in here," she said,

coming back to the overturned dresser. "This mess happened when he forced the door." She gestured over her shoulder at the unmade bed and pile of dirty laundry. "That mess is normal."

Jamie smiled. Marissa never apologized for her lack of housekeeping. At times, he even believed that she wore the trait as a badge of honor. Her mother, she'd said, had devoted her life to waxing the linoleum and polishing the sinks.

Seeing the grin, Marissa pursed her lips at him. *No comments from the peanut gallery.*

One of the cops, O'Connor, scribbled in his notebook. "You sure nothing's missing in here?"

She surveyed the closet again. A gold cross necklace was clasped between her palms, the chain looped around one delicate wrist. "Doesn't look like it."

The cop asked Jamie to help him right the dresser. After it was back on its legs, drawers askew, he said to Marissa, "Check the underwear drawer."

Jamie blurted, *"What?"*

"We get a lot of weirdos," O'Connor explained matter-of-factly. "They like to take souvenirs."

Marissa screwed up her face and opened a couple of the drawers wider. Jamie glimpsed molded plum satin bra cups and frilly silk pastels. She had a lot of lingerie.

A tangled black thong had spilled over the edge. It dangled off one knob, so impossibly tiny it looked like Johnny Depp's eye patch. Both men stared, until Marissa casually scooped up the garment and tossed it in a drawer. "There. All unmentionables accounted for."

"How can you tell?" Jamie asked. His scalp was hot.

She gave him a sidelong look. A small tease of a smile. "I know when my panties have been touched."

Jamie made a choking sound.

The officer snorted.

Marissa sailed out of the room. Harry darted after her. "The thief must not have gotten to the bedroom before I came home and interrupted him. He was looking for something specific and he hadn't found it."

"But you don't know what?" asked the other cop, who'd been examining the locks on the front door. "He popped this, picked the dead bolt, then snapped the chain. Probably took less 'n five minutes."

"You're getting new locks," Jamie said. "One of those huge iron bars that go right across the door. Maybe a moat. With crocodiles."

"I'll call a locksmith in the morning. Then a zoo." Marissa toed the items scattered near the door. "Can I touch these?" The cop shrugged. "Because the guy said he wanted something I brought back from vacation, and other than my laundry…" She picked up a straw purse. "This is it."

Jamie looked into the emptied purse. "What's it?"

"My passport." She found it on the floor. "The camera. A magazine. Odd bits and pieces that don't mean a thing as far as I can tell."

The cop loomed. "This was no ordinary break-in. Nothing's missing. Not your jewelry. Not the TV or other electronics. Do you keep cash in the house?"

Marissa shook her head. "Not much to speak of. I had my wallet with me."

Jamie had retrieved the pieces of the camera. "You might be able to get this fixed. The film is ruined though. You won't have any pictures of your trip."

"Not that I *want* to remember it," Marissa said wryly, "but I loaded a fresh roll after I got home." She waved a hand at the broken pieces. "You can toss that out. I needed a new digital camera anyway."

"So we've got minor damage and nothing stolen," the other policeman said. "Not much to go on, I'm afraid, Miss Suarez."

"What about fingerprints?" She put a hand to her throat and shuddered. "Damn, that's right. He wore gloves."

Jamie moved closer, patting her back when what he really wanted was to stuff her in a bank vault under twenty-four-hour guard.

"And you didn't see his face," the officer reiterated. He'd already said there was little hope of an arrest.

"No, but I can tell you that he was a drinker who needed to see the dentist. Not much to go on." Marissa shook her head, then suddenly brightened. "Oh! I forgot to say there was a second guy, at the bottom of the fire escape. He looked up at me. I saw his face. If he was the lookout, he wasn't a very good one because he was as surprised to see me as I was to see him." Jamie squeezed her hand. "And it was strange, because something about him was familiar."

"Like you might have known him?" O'Connor asked hopefully.

"No-o-o, not really. But I could have seen him around the neighborhood."

"Casing the joint," Jamie said, trying to make her smile.

O'Connor was all business. "That might be. Give me a description, ma'am. Height, weight, distinguishing characteristics."

"That's not so easy." Marissa frowned. "It was dark. There were shadows. And he was dressed in black."

"Race?"

"Caucasian. His face was pale. Narrow, with sharp features, so I'd say he was not very heavy. He had dark eyes and stubble."

"Visible tattoos?"

"Not that I noticed."

"Could you identify him from a mug shot?"

"I can try."

"Come by the precinct. I'll set you up." O'Connor gave her a card. "Here's my number, for, uh, you know."

Not *all* business, Jamie noted. The man's face was getting ruddy and he kept glancing at her legs.

"Thanks," Marissa said easily. She was accustomed to men stumbling over their tongues around her.

The cop tugged at his equipment-laden belt. No Freudian meaning there. "Do you have a place to stay?"

Jamie said, a little too loudly, "She does." Marissa smiled at him, the slightly swollen look of her lips triggering his renewed arousal. He wished the police would hurry up and finish.

Muscles in the officer's jaw bunched as he looked between them. "Gotcha."

Marissa showed them to the door. "I'll be in touch about the mug shots." They insisted she should come in as soon as possible, while her memory was fresh.

"We'll go together to the police station, but first we're calling a locksmith," Jamie said as soon as the officers were gone. "Seriously."

She rubbed her neck. "Let's get some sleep first."

Sleep. Jamie's heart dropped.

But she was right, of course. She'd been traumatized. She needed to rest, recover. He'd waited this long, he could wait another night, even though he suspected she'd change her mind about making love with him. If a short delay was all it took, then she was too unsure and becoming lovers wouldn't have been right anyway.

So he told himself. His semihard dick wasn't as understanding.

He shifted. *Think about something else, bud. Anything but how stupid you were to put the brakes on when she'd been raring to go.*

"Your suitcase," he said.

"My suitcase?"

"Where is it?"

"Under the bed." She rolled her lip between her teeth, blinking in thought. "Jamie! Do you think the mugger— the one on the street—was after my suitcase? Mine, specifically, I mean." She clasped his arm, jogging it a little. "He could even be the same person that was here tonight!"

"That's possible. Let's go see." They hurried back to the bedroom.

"It's still here," she said, pulling the bag out from beneath the bed. "Empty." She sank down onto her knees and flipped it open to show him. Harry immediately appeared to jump into it, sniffing the corners and butting his head against the flap. "I dumped the suitcase in here when I got home, but the next day I took everything out so the damp swimsuits wouldn't funk it up. See?" She made a face. "I'm not a total loss in the domestic department."

He'd seen her in a bikini and *funky* wasn't the word. Neither was domestic goddess. Just *goddess.*

"So what else was in the suitcase?" Harry was rubbing his ears against the zipper.

"Nothing but dirty clothes and a few pairs of shoes. I packed light."

"The mugger didn't know that. I think you're right about him. Too much of a coincidence if the incidents were unrelated."

"So they've made two attempts." She leaned her head against the bed. "I just don't get it. What do they want from me?"

Jamie sat and pulled her up beside him, disturbed by her fragility. For all the kick boxing and Pilates classes, she was a featherweight. It was up to him to keep her safe.

"Let's go over it again. What did you bring back from the islands? There must have been some item you've forgotten. A souvenir maybe?"

"I wish I could produce a tiki god with a diamond embedded inside." She shook her head. "But the only thing I bought on Grand Cayman was the straw purse. I needed a beach carry-all. That *can't* be what the thief wanted. He threw it aside."

"Okay, so what did the burglar say, exactly?"

She went quiet, mulling it over before finally answering. "He asked 'Where is it?' I didn't know what he meant. I brought it home, he said."

Jamie tried to examine the puzzle from another angle. "Then it's possible the vacation had nothing to do with this?"

"It *has* to. I had the impression—" She made a sound of frustration. "Let me think. I swear he said something about me bringing it back from vacation." There was a pause, then suddenly her head came up. "The airport! His exact words were that I brought it from the airport." She dropped her voice, quoting. "And 'We know what you did.' Does that make any sense?"

Not to Jamie. "It's almost as if they think you smuggled something in. Call it the tiki god theory."

She tilted her chin. "So I'm Latin. That makes me look like a drug mule?"

He touched her cheek. "Marissa, full of grace."

"Don't charm me. I'd rather be mad than scared."

"There are other emotions."

"Like what?"

He knew what his body wanted him to say, but Marissa was first in his thoughts. "You should feel safe, secure. Comfortable." His fingers brushed through her hair, combing the shining strands into a ponytail laid across her shoulder. The amber-flecked fire in her eyes dimmed as she relaxed, leaning toward him with a soft sigh.

He allowed himself a moment to breathe in her scent, before nudging her with his nose. "Hey, babe. Pack a few belongings and let's get out of here. You're staying at my place."

"All right." So compliant, for Marissa. "I need to leave a note for Shandi."

"Shandi?"

Marissa winced. "Yes, she's still staying with me."

"What happened to the lice and cockroaches?" he teased, before an odd thought hit him. "Where *is* Shandi?"

"We were out together. She took off with a guy. I don't expect her back for hours, if at all, but I want to leave a note anyway."

"Oh. Of course."

Marissa had gone to the closet. She pulled a hanger, frowning at him over her shoulder. "What does that tone mean?"

There were things about Shandi that Marissa didn't know. She wasn't a friend to count on, especially around men. Jamie had never thought it was his place to tell Marissa that. Not only because he'd rather gouge out his own eyes than see her hurt. He'd figured that Marissa already knew her friend's character quite well and was choosing to overlook the negatives. Despite the toughness she projected, she believed in the essential goodness of human nature.

He evaded. "Just that it might be smart to get your keys back."

"She already turned them over."

"Oh." And the lock had been picked, which was proof of nothing except that the burglar didn't have keys.

"Again with the 'oh.'" Marissa stared, clearly astounded. "Are you suspecting *Shandi* now?"

"She's not the most reliable person, and she always needs money."

"You're way off the mark. If she'd wanted to rob me, she could have emptied the apartment while I was on vacation."

"But you came back early, right?"

Marissa threw a dress at him. With the heavy wood hanger still in it.

He batted it down. "All right, I'm sorry. I was only trying to figure this out. Don't hang me for it."

"Ha, ha." She went to a lingerie drawer, grabbed a couple of skimpy little silk things and balled them in her hand. "You catch Harry and then let's go."

No pajamas, Jamie thought as he chirruped for the cat. And he had only the sofa bed for them to share. It was going to be a long time till morning.

SOME DISTANCE WAS PUT between them by the business of rearranging his place, getting another pillow, a fresh towel, a bar of soap. Sitting and soothing Harry while Marissa took a quick shower worked on Jamie, as well. He managed to subdue and corral his rampaging lust.

Until she walked out of the bathroom, blotting her damp hair with a towel, wearing a tiny pink silk top and even tinier bottoms. Their frilled edge lay along the crease of her leg, lifting along the curve of her bottom when she bent and tousled her hair. Straightening, she flung it past her shoulders like a girl in a shampoo commercial. Silk shimmered over her conspicuously pointy nipples.

"Thanks for the shower. I feel so much better!"

He grunted. Harry jumped from his lap and went to twine himself around Marissa's legs. Lucky cat.

"Where's your sleep shirt? The big, baggy one?"

She blinked. "Dirty clothes pile."

"Want a T-shirt? Sweats?" *A parka.* "You're going to be cold."

She glanced at the sofa bed, the extra blankets he'd gathered. "I'm sure you'll keep me warm."

"You know what you're doing to me, right?"

Her lips pursed into a tight smile. "Of course."

He sighed heavily. "But I'm not supposed to start anything."

Or was he?

She returned her towel to the bathroom, switching off the light before coming back. The apartment turned a dense black. He waited for his eyes to adjust, picking out Marissa's slender form standing beside the bed.

"Thus far," she said, "you've exhibited formidable control."

"Ah, so this is payback."

"Would I be that devious?"

"Hell, yes."

She laughed, agreeing. "Sorry. I'm fresh out of flannel pajamas."

"No problem." He got up and flicked on a bedside

lamp. "Hope you don't mind if I strip down. I put out extra blankets for you, but they'll make me hot if I wear too much to bed." He stripped off the top of the pajamas he'd put on for purposes of modesty and protection, leaving only the bottoms, the drawstring tied loosely so they hung low on his hips. He stretched, flexing his chest muscles, then worked his shoulders back and forth.

Marissa pretended to fluff pillows, but she was watching.

He rubbed below his navel. "Right or left?"

"Huh?"

He rested his hands on his hips. "Do you sleep on the right side or the left?"

"Oh, right, I suppose." She dragged her eyes up from the tent puffing out below his waistband. "Actually, I sleep all over. I'm restless. This bed is small. I might end up sprawled on top of you."

"I've slept under worse conditions."

Her eyes narrowed, but she got into bed without further comment. She stretched out flat, balancing near the right edge. The blankets were spread neatly over her, pulled up to her chest. She kept her hands outside them, folded atop her rib cage.

She closed her eyes. Smiled serenely. "Thank you for coming to my rescue. Good night."

That was it? *Arrgh.*

Moving like an old man, he lowered himself to the bed. With careful positioning, he was able to avoid touching her. The sofa bed's springs squeaked and groaned, the edge of the thin mattress curling inward as if it wanted to throw them together. He tensed up and clung to his perch.

Platitudes filled his brain.

Steady on.

Take it easy.

Don't rush.

But his usual mantra wasn't working.

He remembered how he'd saved for his first guitar when he was fourteen, a limited-edition Gibson acoustic that he'd spotted in a music shop. Too young for a regular job, he'd earned the money by lawn mowing, snow shoveling, dog walking. A year it had taken him. Flashy electric guitars had come and gone through the store, but the Gibson had waited for him, its honey-colored wood sweetly curved and polished.

And when he'd finally had the money—or most of it; he'd gone to the shop with the intention of setting up a payment plan for the remainder—the guitar was no longer there. It had been sold only days before.

Eventually he'd bought a similar guitar. A newer, better one, the shop owner had said.

But it wasn't the same. He'd coveted that Gibson. And remembered, even now, the pleasure of the one time he'd played her, hair falling in his face, fumbling fingers in the corner of the shop, strumming a simple song.

So he knew from experience that once wasn't enough.

Yet it was better than nothing.

Better than waiting too long and losing his chance because he'd dreamed too big.

"JAMIE, are you sleeping?"

His voice came out of the dark. "No."

Marissa smiled to herself. He'd answered so fast that she knew he'd been waiting for her to give him a sign. But on top of everything else she'd been thinking about his off-base suspicions of Shandi and he deserved to suffer, just a little. Shandi was selfish and a mooch, but she wasn't a thief.

"Me, neither. I'm stifling under all these blankets." Marissa flung off two layers. "Much better."

"Just right, is it, Goldilocks?"

"As a matter of fact, yes." She brushed her leg against his, to be certain he was thinking about her being half-naked only inches away. "Sorry."

Bad idea. The electric touch sent a shivery tingle through her. The heat of him clung to her like a force field, entreating her to roll over and curl up into his warmth. She wanted to dive into him like a pool, swallow him like hot fudge.

"That's okay, just don't do it again," he reprimanded.

She slid her foot over. Touched their toes.

"That was on purpose."

"I'm weak," she whispered.

He scoffed.

"I am! When it comes to—" She stopped and thought. Men were her downfall, but not really. While she'd made mistakes, she hadn't actually suffered for them. With Jamie though…

Everything would be different.

High stakes, big risk.

Oh, please! Cut the drama. Get over yourself and just jump him already. The world didn't come crashing to a halt because you lusted after your best friend, and it won't when you shag him, either.

Besides, added the impulsive Marissa, *he looks too good in his bare chest and bare feet and candy-striped pj's to pass up.*

The little show he'd put on before getting into bed had worked. She was revved up with nowhere to go.

When she'd seen how thick and full his penis had grown inside the loose cotton pajama bottoms, her tongue had curled against her teeth, trying to get out. She'd wanted to catch him by the drawstring, drag him near, drop the pants with one quick tug, take him in her hands, in her mouth, taste him on her tongue—

I want to have sex with my friend, Jamie, she said to herself, testing the idea. *Jamie, my lover.*

That sounded fine. Extremely fine.

Ever since her return from the islands, she'd seen him with new eyes. Unlike the men she'd been dating, Jamie was strong in body *and* mind.

Especially in character. She'd underestimated how much she valued an honest, upstanding man.

She'd intended to tease him, but lust was taking hold. Taking over. The depth and strength was revealing when, for three years, she'd rarely lingered on his potential as a lover. Now that was all she could think of.

He felt the same way, so at least she wouldn't have to suffer the indignity of craving and longing and nerves. Not for long.

"We have to talk," he said.

The pit of her stomach dropped like a stone. "That sounds ominous."

"No, it's only picking up where we stopped."

She reached for his hand and placed it over her breast. "You stopped here."

For one brief moment his fingers closed over her nipple and she felt the tug travel straight through her. Then he yanked his hand away.

"We have to decide where we want this to go," he said in a robotic monotone. Even so, the desire in his voice was rough and deep. Embedded.

She moved restlessly, finally letting herself roll into the center of the bed, her nerve endings jumping and sparking as she brushed against his solid body. He was hot all over. His upper arm pressed against one of her taut nipples and she almost leaped out of her skin. She'd always been sensitive there; now she was on a hair trigger.

"You're too careful," she said. Even without the extra blankets, the heat between them was thick and seething.

"You're too impulsive."

"I haven't been with you."

"And why is that, do you think?"

"Because I didn't know it would be this way."

"What way?"

She closed her eyes, breathing through her nose. He was going to make her say it. "I didn't know I would want you this much."

"You want me." He said it with wonder, making her twinge inside. The man had no idea of his immense appeal.

She stretched like a cat, then braced her heels to push higher against the pillows, freeing her upper torso from the tangled sheet. She tipped her head near his, letting her breath blow across his bare shoulder to his cheek. "Just as much as you want me."

His eyes shone at her in the dark. She heard him swallow. He was a goner, but stubborn. "What happened to the worry about keeping our friendship?"

"I realized something, hauling ass up the fire escape." She clasped his hand. "You mean more to me than friendship. It was dumb to think that we should stop there."

"But you said—"

"And *you* said being lovers will enhance our friendship."

"Now we're arguing each other's sides."

She sat up and pulled off her camisole in one fluid motion, then, when he didn't move except for the hitch of his chest, she leaned over, practically on top of him, her arms braced on either side of his shoulders. Her breasts swayed inches above his face.

She nipped at his mouth, moving away when he tried to reach for a real kiss. "That must mean we're of one mind."

He made a grunting sound. "If you're sure, I have no more arguments."

His fingertips ran up the inside of her arms, trailing fire like a comet. She inhaled sharply. "*Are* you sure?" he asked.

She had to be honest, at least with herself. *For the moment,* I am sure.

Tomorrow was another question. Her head swirled at the thought of next week, next month. A year from now. She couldn't imagine not having him in her life, so she didn't try.

His palms passed over her breasts, barely grazing them. She lifted a leg to slip astride him. Her spine pushed in, pressing her lower belly against the hot satin of his flat stomach. A heady sense of fullness and congestion pooled where their bodies met. She rubbed against him, her eyes rolling back in her head as she let herself revel in the moment of first seduction, more than ready to experience all of it—Jamie's fingers, Jamie's tongue, Jamie's cock….

She lifted up a little, soothing the burn. Her thighs were spread wide. Against the thin silk of the tap pants, the lips of her sex had become ripe and swollen, flowing with the honeyed warmth of her arousal.

She was open. Ready to let him in. To trust the leaping faith that they were doing what was right.

"Jamie," she said. "Make love to me."

He took her face between his hands. "Now *that's* what I call asking the right way."

Her reward was a kiss that started with a swoop of swirling tongue and quickly deepened to a hot open-mouthed passion. There was no longer any question of *Should I?* or *Shouldn't I?* No parry and thrust. No retreat. They grasped greedily at each other, plunging recklessly into the sexual abandon that they'd put off for too long.

7

JAMIE RAN HIS HANDS down Marissa's back. He was dazzled. He was dazed. He had to keep touching her to make himself believe this was really happening.

She let out a squeak of surprise when his palms plunged past the skimpy pants to cup her bare bottom. Her thighs tensed, lifting her higher as she tilted to thrust her firm, curved ass hard against his hands.

He was knotted up so tight it was an effort to speak. "Can we have the light? I want to see you." He intended to memorize her.

She nodded, dropping to all fours so she could reach the lamp. The light made her skin golden. With her face hidden in the sweep of long black hair, she rocked back onto her heels, her smooth curves sliding beneath his fingers. He lightly brushed them down the crack of her bottom, meaning the caress to be discreet until she opened her legs wider and he touched her hot slick center.

They both jerked, as if he'd plugged his finger into a light socket.

Marissa tossed back her head. Her teeth had bitten into her lower lip. "Touch me again," she said in a hoarse voice.

"Don't be so impatient." He clenched his hands against her thighs to hide the shaking.

She watched him with her head hung low, eyes black with a glittering arousal. Her perfect breasts were suspended above his face, the tight little nipples pointed at his mouth, veritably tempting him to take a taste.

"Hold still." He stroked upward from her hips, along the thin, sensitive skin over her ribs to the sweetly rounded weight of her breasts. As much as he longed to, he didn't linger there, only skimmed the points of her nipples, circled her shoulders, then continued along the path back the other way. Sensations coursed from his palms and up his arm, begging to be savored, but he didn't stop. One hand coasted along the outside of her thigh until it caught at the back of her knee. The flat of his other hand reached past her navel and smooth belly to the neat patch of fur revealed as her pants slipped off her hips. Her pelvis tilted, welcoming him.

The air in his lungs grew sharp as his fingers found her cleft. He gripped her thigh steady to give him even better access, but there was no real need. Her knees were spread as far as they could go and yet still keep her upright. She was making small, excited noises. Rocking her hips.

"Shh, slow down," he said, trying to settle her.

"I don't think that's possible." But she took a deep breath that dropped her shoulders low enough for her to rub her cheek against his. She made a murmuring sound of encouragement.

Slow down? Who was he kidding? Tension had

strung his nerves taut as a bow. His blood was charged, pulsing inside him with demands that he had to fight to delay. He was determined to take his time. He wanted to give her all the pleasure that he could.

The finger he eased between the pouting lips of her sex was instantly coated by the slippery warmth of her viscous flow. She was aroused. Highly aroused.

His masculine pride surged, like the first time he'd brought a woman to orgasm. There was no doubt in him that seeing—*feeling*—Marissa come apart under his command would outweigh the sum of all previous experiences. He was as eager as an eighteen-year-old, wild to have her long legs wrapped around him, to spill himself in her tight, clinging body. Her memories of other boyfriends would burn to ashes when she came like she'd never come before.

She'd closed her eyes. He looked at her face, silent and focused. Wanting to give her more than sexual pleasure, he gently urged her over onto her back, enabling him to press closer, gathering her in a one-armed hug while still working a playful finger in and out of her.

The silence in the studio apartment was broken only by the occasional softly feminine moan and the distant racket from the street of delivery trucks and early dawn copter traffic. Anticipation hung in the air, so heavy he could taste it.

Marissa wriggled in his embrace, kicking away her remaining piece of lingerie. "Stop being a tease," she said. "Touch me there." As if she were shy, she pressed her face to his neck. Seconds later she was kissing and nibbling at his throat.

Obediently he stroked through the intimate folds to rub against the hard button of her clit. Even though she'd asked for it, she stiffened with another of the undrawn gasps, scraping his carotid with her teeth. He eased up, caressing her inner thighs instead, giving her inflamed senses a minute to recover.

She let out a big sigh. Her arms went around his neck. "I can't take this."

"You can." He kissed the top of her head. "And so will I. We'll take it all the way."

And you'll take me, he thought, his mind dark with the erotic image of burying himself in the tiny opening he'd barely fit two fingers into. Primal urges were shattering his plan to love her slowly and completely, as if they had all the time in the world. Perhaps all along he'd been worried about the opposite—that they would have only one night and he would have to make it last forever.

Marissa's lips moved against his throat. "I don't want to come this way," she insisted even though she was trembling under his touch. A couple of hard strokes would bring her off. "I want you—" she nipped at his ear "—inside me."

"I don't intend to give you only one orgasm."

She made a sound of amusement. "You should have told me about your great skill in this department. If I'd known, we'd have become lovers years ago."

"What a fool I've been." He smiled down at her. "From now on, I'll try to be more boastful."

They kissed. Marissa's mouth was soft, loose. So was the rest of her, now that he'd switched to slow caresses that wandered over her entire body. She moved languorously beneath his mouth, her hair fanned across the pillow. He could drink from her like this for hours and be satisfied.

Almost satisfied.

She covered his wandering hand with her own, lazily directing him to her breasts. "They ache."

"I can fix that." He put his mouth to her breasts, where her skin was so pale it glowed in the dusky room, and dabbled them with small, wet kisses. She tasted the way she smelled—of warm, ripe woman, a little spicy, a little sweet. Taut brown nipples rolled beneath his tongue, popping up against his lips. No longer able to resist, he drew on first one, then the other, sucking them deep into his mouth, back and forth, licking and nibbling until she dug her fingers compulsively into his shoulders, thrashing her legs against the sheets.

He pulled away. "Better?"

Her black pupils were rimmed by the thinnest ring of color. "Worse." She gulped. "Much worse. In fact, so much worse that I demand you keep practicing."

He surveyed her beautifully aroused body, slender as a blade of golden grass. "Practice, huh? Well, I was never very disciplined about my music lessons, but I loved to sit for hours on the seawall and strum my guitar." Luckily she couldn't read his mind, because all he could think of was how he'd like to make her tight pussy sing a vibrato.

"And how would you play *me?*" She put a hand over her dark tuft, the knowing tone telling him that lately she'd become quite aware of how his mind worked.

"With—" *With love.*

He stopped himself just in time, withholding because he remembered how she'd disdained men who mistook the first exciting rush of sex for love, to the point where they dithered over her like syrup-sopped romantics.

She *claimed* to prefer meeting her sexual needs in a straightforward manner. But he'd also seen how her gaze lingered on loving couples on the street, almost guiltily, especially with the greeting-card moments like seventy-year-olds holding hands and a husband kissing his wife's pregnant tummy bulge.

Because he knew Marissa so well, he also knew her secret: she believed in true love.

So did he, a conviction that had grown stronger in the past few years. The words wanted to burst out of him, but he settled for enfolding her in another embrace. For now, he would have to show her how he felt. That, at last, she would accept.

"I will play you like a symphony," he said, and proceeded to show her that even though his garage-band days were long gone, he hadn't lost his touch.

"THIS IS WEIRD," Marissa said from the huddle of pillows where she'd burrowed in an attempt to escape his maddeningly meticulous hands. She needed a moment to regain her breath before she lost control of her body altogether.

Jamie looked up, crestfallen.

"Not you!" Certainly not him. He'd done everything right, if too carefully—kissing and stroking every nook and cranny as if he'd flunk his finals in sex ed if he neglected a millimeter of skin.

"Are you thinking of the break-in?"

That was at the back of her mind, but… "No."

"Is it because we're too familiar?" he said. "Pretend I'm a stranger."

She kissed him. "You'll never be a stranger."

"Then pretend we've done this a hundred times before."

"I like that it's our first time," she confessed, feeling girlish. A blush warmed her face. "But then there's our audience." She peeked past the edge of a rumpled blanket. Sally stood at the foot of the bed, watching them with a big doggie grin, her tongue lolling. "I prefer if the heavy breathing comes from you."

"Sally. Shoo." He kicked at the air. "Go on. Shoo."

The dog laid her head on the bed. Big brown eyes stared at them.

Under the covers, Jamie's thumb rubbed across Marissa's nipple. "She won't tell anyone what she sees."

"She'll tell Harry." Marissa lay flat, pulling the sheet past her face. "They'll have a big discussion about our technique."

Jamie crawled out of bed. "I'll shut her in the bathroom, okay?"

"With a Chewy Bone!" she called after him.

He was back in thirty seconds, tossing a strip of condom packets on the bedside table before sliding in behind her. "Now where were we?"

"Um." She squirmed her bottom. He pressed against her, his erection stabbing her in the small of the back. "I believe you have a bone for me, too," she said, and giggled. "Oh, man, that was so cheesy. I must be nervous. Whatever that feels like."

He made an adjustment, touching her lower where her thighs pressed together, and she no longer wanted to laugh. Her stomach was jumping, however, and she knew very well that it was nerves. They were about to go to a place in their relationship where there'd be no turning back.

"You're sure this isn't weirding you out?" he whispered.

"Surprisingly, no. But let's not dwell on that or it *will* get awkward."

His hands were in her hair, lifting it. "No more talking," he said against her nape. "Just kissing."

She shivered, fighting to lie still under his wandering hands as he lavished her with adoration. It seemed that he'd been caressing her for an hour. She was so ready that even her follicles were vibrating, but she'd wanted him to have his own pace.

Typically, he'd given little thought to himself. By now, he had to be hurting something fierce.

He flinched when she rubbed against his stiff penis. "Babe. Don't do that yet."

She turned to face him. "Let me touch you."

"I'm afraid I'll—*urgh*." He gritted his teeth.

She'd reached past the waistband of his pajama pants. At her first tentative touch, he tossed his head like a wild horse.

Marissa hummed with enjoyment. His groin was hot, fragrant with musk. She wrapped her hand around his shaft, rubbed her thumb around the rim, the slickened tip. He jerked so violently she lost her grasp.

Mercy! Such unbridled passion. Her inner muscles squeezed down on a bolt of anticipation. Jamie would fill her so well. She slithered closer, shoving his pajamas past his lean hips.

He caught her elbow. "I'm telling you, that's dangerous."

"Not if you're inside me."

"But I—"

"Shh. I know what you were doing." She gave him a deep kiss. "And you did it so well—" biting his jaw, strumming her tongue over the strained cords in his neck "—that if I don't have you, *right now,* I'm going to explode." She nuzzled the hollow where his pulse throbbed. His unleashed hard-on twitched against her belly.

"Oh-hh…okay." He looked embarrassed. "I wanted to do this right."

"Dork." She got right up next to him, no inch of skin unmatched. "Don't you know that you're *so* right? Without doing a thing." Sliding her leg over his, she felt the textures of his rough hair and taut muscle with her inner thigh. "But we need to find our rhythm together."

"Ride this." He thrust his thigh forward, seating it against her vulva. She squirmed, opening herself. The contact on her clit was a shock, riveting her with a concentrated blast of pure, fiery sensation. His groin was a forge, his erection as hard and hot as a bar of steel sizzling against her most intimate flesh. Waves of heat rolled through her. He reached for one of the packets and she thought that they would melt the condom for sure.

Somehow he managed to roll the rubber on, even with her trying to crawl up inside him. She was almost weeping with the pressure and tension and need.

"Hold on to me, babe."

She gripped his shoulders. He nudged her over onto her back without losing the contact. He stroked several fingers through her wetness, plunging them inside before spreading her to accept the sheathed head of his penis. She dug her heels in, lifted her pelvis.

"In me," she said. Gasping, grabbing.

"Shh." Jamie framed her face, gentling her with his steadiness. She welcomed his weight as he sank partway onto her. And into her. "Look at me."

She opened her eyes. He was looking straight at her. No awkwardness, no hesitation. Warmth and wonder in his expression, caring in his touch.

The truth smacked her. *She* was the one who felt unsure, especially about this…this feeling of—

Her lids slammed shut. Her body clamped on his. "Ride me."

A groan tore loose from Jamie's throat as he finally surrendered. He pushed all the way inside her, hot steel and pulsing flesh, sweet glide and delicious friction, filling her with more than his body even though she tried not to think about what that meant.

But her body had another agenda. She opened to him. Yielded. Accepted.

He was deep. So deep.

She shuddered with her palms on his firm butt and her legs splayed, keeping him right there, unmoving as her eyes rolled back in her head and her mind expanded to absorb the reality of being Jamie's lover.

"Marissa," he said into her neck. Prayerfully.

She breathed his name. "Jamie."

His head bumped her chin. She sank a hand into his thick curly hair as he dipped lower. His tongue was a warm, wet lash on her skin, lapping hard at her nipples until she had no choice but to take the next step in their dance.

First her shoulders swayed, then her hips. He rocked into her, not quite thrusting, but moving just enough so that she felt him throbbing inside her. A delicious sensation. She hooked a leg around him and arched her back, lifting her breasts into the wet heat of his mouth. Passion rushed her veins and her nerve endings swelled and tingled, making her skin so sensitive it was almost painful.

He released her breast, found her mouth, filled it with his tongue. She tightened on him and he reared back, his face turning fierce as he thrust and thrust again, giving her all of himself. And then he was whispering to her, a chain of exciting, forbidden words—how hot she was, how wet, how tight—all of it leading her deeper into uncharted territory.

She shook, on the verge of coming apart. Jamie knew what she needed. He hugged her as he pulled out, so slowly it was excruciating, then tightened his hold even more when he drove back in. A scintillating pleasure broke inside her and then she really was coming, but not apart.

She was consummate. She was whole. And Jamie was right there with her.

A pressure built behind her lids, at the back of her throat. She held it at bay, sinking her nails into his shoulders as he pumped hard and fast. A deep warmth blossomed from the point of their coupling, washing over her in a swirling wave. She gave in to it, losing herself in the rush and movement and pleasure, losing herself in the moment that felt as though it should never end.

Jamie slipped out of her. Not wanting to let go, she twined him in her legs and arms. He rested on his elbows, his hands in her hair, kissing her face, his tongue tickling as he licked away the tears that had spilled from her eyes without her realizing it.

"That was hot," she said.

He wouldn't let her diminish the act. "That was beautiful."

She pushed her face into the crook of his arm. "It was."

"Still is," he said, kissing her and softly rubbing his face against her cheek, making her think of the cat.

She lifted her head. "Was Harry under the bed all this time? He must be traumatized." Even though their pets were familiar with each other, the cat had fled for safety as soon as she'd released him inside the door to the apartment.

"Nope." Jamie gestured with his head. "Look over there."

The room was only dimly lit, but Harry was visible, a

pale shape ensconced on the easy chair opposite their sofa bed. "Wow," Marissa said. "He let us be? You're lucky you don't have cat scratches up and down your back."

"Who says I don't?"

She checked her polished nails. "Gosh. Did I hurt you?"

"Not a bit."

She stroked his shoulder and felt him flinch. "Battle wounds."

"Do I get a Purple Heart?"

"Let's hope not." Better to skim away from that area, which could easily digress to hearts and flowers when she—*he*—was feeling so sated. "It must be the different apartment."

"What?"

"Harry. Usually, if I'm with a guy, in a romantic situation, Harry lets his displeasure be known."

"Is that why you rarely bring men home?"

So he'd noticed that. She'd always told herself that she liked her privacy and that was why she kept her home life separate from her sex life. But at least some of her reticence to share herself with even the long-term boyfriends was because she didn't want to involve either Harry or, she must admit, Jamie.

She summoned a humorous tone. "I'm careful about who I introduce Harry to, that's all." Jamie *had* met anyone who lasted long enough to be called a boyfriend. He was scrupulously friendly to them, too, even though she could tell that he wasn't ever entirely approving. Not unlike Harry.

She gave Jamie's back a pat, enjoying these moments

of slightly sticky closeness a little too much regardless of the way he was making her reevaluate. "I need to wash up, but I'm too lazy to move."

"Me, too," he said, but a minute later he got out of bed, pajamas in hand, and disappeared into the bathroom. Soon he returned with a damp washcloth and a towel. The dog was on his heels.

"What's this?" she asked, flicking on a second sofa lamp.

He blinked at the sudden light, then smiled, making no explanation other than, "I know you."

She knew him, too. He'd often teased her about her propensity for meticulous grooming. From work to workout to bed, she sometimes took three showers a day. After sex, she was the one to bolt for the bathroom, and often even zoom out of the man's apartment with excuses about having to get up early for work. Paul had liked that about her. He'd said she thought like a man, which he considered a compliment. Maybe she had also…at the time.

She scoffed at herself. As if "the time" had been so long ago.

But maybe it was. Some days, even hours, meant more than others.

She reached for the washcloth, but Jamie demurred. "It's late. Early, I mean. You're tired. Let me."

She *was* sleepy. That was why she gave in, lying back and letting him take care of her. He started with her arms, sliding the damp cloth along them and then over to her breasts. He washed her there with careful attention. She propped up her heavy lids, needing to watch his face for…for…

She didn't know what. How could she be suspicious of his thoughtfulness?

He remained efficient. Careful, gentle, but not lascivious, even when he lifted her legs, swiping the warm wet cloth across her inner thighs, then between them. A frisson went through her.

He was applying the towel, drying her off. His concentration was almost total, only the dark glint in his eyes hinting at the intimacy of his actions.

"That feels good." She sat up and unfolded the T-shirt, slipping it over her head while he straightened the sheets and blanket, even plumped her pillow.

She snuggled in. He switched off the lights, climbing in beside her. He was reaching for her when a heavy weight thumped onto the bed. Sally plopped her big furry body between them. Her tail waved hopefully.

"Hello." Marissa stroked the retriever's velvety head.

"She usually sleeps with me," Jamie confessed.

"Does that make me the other woman?"

He settled back, one arm propped behind his head. He fingered Sally's ear. "The other female, maybe."

"Sally will share, won't you, girl?"

The dog's tail thumped the blanket. She was in bliss, with both of them stroking behind her ears, scratching her chin, rubbing under her collar to the ruff of silky golden hair.

"Double petting session," Jamie said. "What a treat."

"We shouldn't be the only ones enjoying ourselves tonight."

"Sweet baby girl," he crooned.

For half a second, Marissa thought he meant her. But he was talking to the dog, working her into soporific ecstasy with his attentions.

Marissa's fingers stilled on the dog's ruff. Her eyes closed. She drifted. Eventually her hand fell away. She tried to rouse herself when the dog nudged at her, but Jamie scolded, "Sally. Go to sleep."

The dog rose and went to the foot of the bed, turning in circles before settling at their feet.

She reached for Jamie with her face until she found his lips. His breath was sweet with toothpaste, and that made her smile. "Thank you."

"What for?"

"Being there for me."

"Where?" He nudged her with his hips. "Here?"

"Are you trying to wake me up?"

"Ah, no. Unless you really can't sleep…"

"Umm." She loved being close to him this way, and felt comforted that they hadn't lost the easy give and take of their friendship. Her feelings were, as he'd said, enhanced. Perhaps there was a small niggling doubt that threatened to bloom into misgivings, but for now she was too lethargic to give it space to grow.

He petted her hip. "Are you still worrying about the burglary?"

"Not so much. But I suppose it is buzzing at the back of my mind."

"It'll be okay. I'll help you get everything straightened up, we'll go to the police station, and the hardware store, and I'll install window grates…."

"Oh, joy. I don't do well in captivity."

"Think of it as keeping out the crazies."

She was drifting away again. "Mmm-hmm."

"It'll be okay," he whispered. "I promise."

She believed him. The last thing she was aware of before she fell asleep was the sensation of Jamie kissing her forehead.

A SHRILL, DEMANDING noise woke Marissa. She groaned and tried to bury her ears in the pillow. No go. The ringing sound wouldn't quit.

She cranked up her head and squinted at the light coming through the windows, then blearily focused on the clock. After 10:00 a.m.

The first day of the rest of her life, so to speak. Her new life as Jamie's—what? Was she now officially his girlfriend?

She knew without a doubt that he'd say so. She, however, wasn't so sure now that the sun, like her defenses, was up.

The persistent noise wasn't Jamie's alarm. It was her cell phone.

She sat up, vaguely remembering Jamie taking the dog out at some point, but he'd come back to bed and was a lump beside her. Sally, too, squeezed in with her big body stretched lengthwise alongside his.

"Answer it," the bigger lump said.

Her bag was at the side of the bed. She pulled out the phone, checked the display, but didn't recognize the number. Manhattan area code. "Hullo?"

"Miss Suarez, this is Sergeant O'Connor of the NYPD"

"Oh. Yes, of course." She pushed her hair out of her face, rubbed her eyes. She was never good at tiptoeing through delicate morning-after situations, so she latched onto the call as a handy excuse. "You want me to come in, do the mug shot thing?"

"That may not be necessary," the cop said, and she could tell by the tone in his voice that he was about to tell her something bad.

Jamie sat up. Sally rolled onto her back with her legs splayed, expecting a belly scratch. "What is it?"

Marissa stopped formulating rationalizations in her mind and concentrated on the telephone call. She held up a finger, shushing Jamie while O'Connor spoke to her. She sputtered out a few questions, but he could give her no real answers, not yet.

With numb fingers, she snapped the phone shut. Being with Jamie had given her a sense of security, but now she saw that she'd only pulled him into a dangerous situation they had no solution for.

"Marissa. Tell me," Jamie commanded with a sense of urgency she'd never heard from him before the past few days.

Her lips had no feeling, but she heard her voice speaking through them. "That was one of the cops from last night. O'Connor. They may have found my burglar."

"That was fast." Jamie thrust a hand through his rumpled hair. "But what's wrong?"

"Well. They want me to come in right away."

"For a lineup?"

"No, a corpse-up." That was a sick thing to say. Was she losing it?

Her eyes darted around a room that suddenly seemed unfamiliar. The Kurt Cobain poster on the back of the door had a torn corner. She'd dog-eared half the books stacked by the armchair, but now they wore strange covers and titles. She could have sworn she'd never seen the guitar in the corner before, even though Jamie had once played "Don't Worry, Be Happy" at the bottom of her fire escape when she'd fumbled a big case at work. Her skin was twitchy. Her tongue felt rough. Even the air she breathed tasted wrong.

She didn't want to look at Jamie, in case he was no longer recognizable either.

Had she made another of her gigantic mistakes?

She swallowed. "I guess I have to go to the morgue, to see if I can identify…" Her teeth clicked together and she swallowed the sour taste in her mouth. The break-in had been bad, but now the situation had become deadly serious, on top of infernally complicated. "To identify the body."

"The body?"

With closed eyes, she reached for Jamie, hoping that she could still find comfort in his presence. Burying her face in his chest, she said, "One of the burglars is dead. They found him a block away, hidden behind a Dumpster. He was stabbed."

8

"GRACIAS, ALEKSEI!" Marissa sang when the waiter arrived with a tray of margarita glasses. He smiled at her when she started passing them out before he could. "Ladies, you don't know how much I needed this lunch." She'd been jumpy at work that morning: wondering if Paul would show up. Fortunately it seemed he'd stayed in the Caymans for the full week.

Three of her girlfriends, Cassandra Richards, Sylvana Ruiz-Dominguez and Trish Spencer, lifted the mango margaritas in toast to Marissa. As they'd been chain-calling since her return from the Caymans, they already knew of the recent developments. The Friday lunch date was the first time they'd had a chance to get together to hear about the details in person. Whether they were more interested in the break and enter or the encounter with Jamie was a toss-up.

"Let's get down to it," Cass said, sipping her drink. "How was he?"

Short toss. Marissa plunked her glass on the table, stalling for time. Telling of other conquests, she'd been generous with details. These were her closest friends and she trusted them. Only Trish was a less frequent lunch participant. As the staff attorney for an old-money foundation that specialized in architectural historic preservation, she often handled out-of-town negotiations and contracts.

"Give us the dirty details," Sylvie encouraged.

Trish's eyes widened. "Do we get measurements, too?" She was a mousy brunette, more reserved than the rest of them about what she called her unexciting love life. She claimed that her big brother Alex had received all the looks, charm and sex appeal in the family.

"Measurements? Naturally." There was no modesty about Sylvie, a Latina bombshell. She gestured with her hands, red nails flashing. "We want all the good stuff." She was the only married woman among them. Seven years and counting, but her sex life was as spicy as they came. "I'm a circumference girl myself."

And she'd quite openly assured them that her husband, Tonio, lived up to her standards. *That* had been a conversation to remember.

"Hmm. Let me think." Marissa gave her friends a sly look. "You know how they say anything over six inches is just for show?"

"Who says that?" Cass demanded.

"Six-inchers," Trish replied deadpan, surprising them.

The four women laughed gaily, drawing looks from the other patrons of the Upper West Side bistro that was their usual midpoint meeting place for workday lunches. The cast of Marissa's friends was often in flux, but she'd connected with a group of up-and-coming professionals during her first months in Manhattan and had come to rely on them to supply the family closeness she missed.

Sylvie probed for details. "Did Jamie exceed expectations?"

Marissa smiled. "Let's just say that on those particular terms, he would give a good show."

Sylvie stirred her drink, eying Marissa behind a swoop of sleek dark hair. Her lips twitched. "And the width?"

"I'm not going there."

"Aw, come on," Cass chided. "Why so discreet?"

Marissa refused with a head shake. "What about you? Tell us how Sam, the cop from Queens, measures up." Cassandra, who'd always claimed to prefer style over substance, had recently become enamored with a working-class man under the most unusual circumstances—out on a ledge, trying to rescue a Hermès scarf.

Cass pressed her palms to her cheeks, unusually bashful. "No comment."

"No fair," Marissa said, but she understood. Part of her wanted to keep the moments with Jamie private and special. But she was also slightly unhinged by the awkwardness between them since the big event. She wanted her friends' advice. And maybe to boast about how good it was, just a little.

"I'm not bagging on you," Cass explained. "Sam and I have a flirtation, that's all."

"But you're taking him to the Hamptons this weekend," Trish pointed out.

"That's business." Cass grinned. "At least for him."

Sam Mason was tracking a jewel thief who preyed on the glitterati. Cassandra planned to introduce him to the hip crowd that she'd courted and befriended in her position as a public relations assistant.

"Let's get back to Marissa and Jamie." Cass looked around the table. "Although we're not surprised they finally got together, are we, girls?"

Sylvie nodded with agreement; she'd always been an advocate of letting chemistry overboil instead of keeping it on a back burner, simmering for a rainy day.

But Trish wasn't so sure. "I expected you to stay the course," she said to Marissa. "Your mind seemed *so* made up that Jamie was only a friend. You even set me up with him!"

Marissa had once persuaded her old law school pal Trish to accept a blind date with Jamie, certain they'd be a perfect match. The two had gone out, but the sparks weren't there. Too much alike, they'd decided, both being brainy, all-around nice people. Trish had reported that Jamie had spent most of their lunch date telling outrageous Marissa stories. She'd avoided examining why, but she'd been secretly pleased.

"I admit it. I was wrong," Marissa said solemnly.

Sylvie's head snapped up. "Regrets already?"

"No, I was wrong to insist that he was only my friend." She sighed. "But I don't know if making him my lover was wise either."

"Aw," Cass said with concern. "Why not?"

Marissa shrugged. "Look at my track record."

"Mine was no better until I met Tonio," said Sylvie.

"Not the same. You weren't friends with him first. With me and Jamie, there are already so many layers to our relationship."

Trish raised her brows. "You say that like it's a bad thing."

"It's not what I'm used to. My affairs are simple and clean. Sex has never been about…" Marissa wrinkled her nose. She couldn't use the *L* word. "About feelings." She put on a shudder. "*Feelings.* Yuck."

"Yes, that sounds like pure torture." Cass was smiling and shaking her head at the same time. "I can't believe you're complaining about having a man who truly cares for you. To use your own words—deal with it."

"You know how that will go." Marissa made a chopping gesture. Previously, she'd had no problem making decisions about what fit where in the grand scheme of her life. She didn't like the waffling and hesitation of the past several days.

Trish was shocked. "You wouldn't dump him!"

A pang bit into Marissa's midsection at the very thought. "Oh, no. But it'd be nice if Jamie would…"

"Stop inserting colors into your black-and-white world?" Sylvie looked almost smug. She'd said all along that Marissa was too controlled.

"Where *does* Jamie stand on all of this?" Cass asked.

Marissa thought the question over. "He was leery at first, but now that we did it, he seems happy."

Sylvie tossed her hands. "Of course! What man wouldn't be happy? He's having sex with a hot girl."

Marissa paused. Sylvie's comment had given her an opening to turn the conversation back in a bawdy direction. Instead, she plunged on. "It's me who can't figure out how to negotiate through the changes."

"You'll find a way," Trish assured her.

Cass, more familiar with Marissa's tendencies, was less certain. "You know," she said, treading carefully, "I have a feeling that you've been given a shot at the real thing."

Marissa had the same feeling. That was a large part of what worried her. She had a plan for her life and falling into the *L* word wasn't on the agenda.

Cass frowned when she saw the doubt in her friend's face. "Don't bollix it up, Mari."

"Easier said than done."

Sylvie gave a saucy wink. "Come what may, at least the sex was good."

"Very," Marissa said with emphasis. Enough with the angst. She was a woman of action. Even when her actions got her into hot water.

Cass straightened the cuff of her peacock-blue Isaac Vincent shirt. A fabulous wardrobe was the most enviable perk of her job with the couture house. "You never did answer the circumference question."

Sylvie smirked. "Does he measure up to Tonio?" Her pet name for her husband was *El Toro*. The bull.

"Hush," Trish warned. "Here comes our waiter."

Marissa waved a hand. "Oh, don't worry. Aleksei's heard it all before."

"Indeed. And most of it from you." Their longtime

waiter distributed salads. Only Sylvie, who was trying to get pregnant, had ordered red meat. London Broil, to build up her blood, she said, although she'd always been an inveterate carnivore.

"How did the actual first move happen?" Trish picked up a fork. "It must have been strange. Like kissing your cousin."

"What's strange is that it wasn't strange at all." Marissa squeezed lemon over her seafood salad. "Jamie came to pick me up at the airport after the disaster with Paul. The moment I saw him, I knew something was different. We clicked in a way we hadn't before. Not for my part, anyway."

"Maybe the disastrous vacation with Paul was the impetus?" Cass suggested.

Sylvie nodded. "Rebound action."

Rebound? Marissa fought against reducing Jamie to that, but there might be an inkling of truth in the comment. Her mood became bleak. "Damn. Did you have to bring up Paul? Thinking of him makes me wonder if I'm fooling myself this time, too." She searched her friends' faces for reassurance. "What if Jamie's just another mistake?"

Before anyone could answer, she went on. "I go around believing my life is under control, that I'm smart, organized, capable. But that's a lie, isn't it?" She frowned, giving herself a good hard look. "My bad choices with men aren't the only clue. Consider the mess in my apartment—it's like the window into my screwed-up psyche."

"Your psyche's not screwed up," said Cass, always loyal.

Trish touched Marissa's arm. "We all feel lost and helpless at times."

"Speak for yourselves," Sylvie said, but then she relented. "I suppose there are moments when I'm not as together as I like to think."

"No." Marissa was on the verge of a full-fledged funk. Perhaps even a wallow in misery. "You're the coolest women I know. I'm the only mess here."

"Give me a break," Cass scoffed. "You know how ditzy I can be." She looked at Trish and Sylvie. "Did I tell you all how freaked out I was about falling eight stories into a giant air bag? I was only lucky that my G-stringed butt didn't wind up on the eleven o'clock news instead of cradled in Sam's hands."

Marissa swirled the dregs of her drink. "The way I hear it, Sam's hands were a news flash all their own." She signaled the waiter. "Aleksei. Another round for my friends."

"Not me," Sylvie said. She patted her flat midriff. "Just in case."

"So we're not the superwomen you believe," Cass re-iterated after they'd distributed the fresh drinks and munched on a few bites of their salads.

"Yes, we are. We're fabulous." Sylvie flashed a huge smile. "Including Marissa."

"Gee, thanks."

Trish nodded in her serious way. "Even fabulous women can make mistakes."

"Preferably enjoyable ones," Cass said. An obviously fond memory—or prospect—lit up her beautiful face. "*Really* enjoyable."

Marissa nibbled a shred of lobster. "Okay. You've convinced me. I'll consider Paul a lesson learned."

"Ugh, no. That sounds so practical. He was an experience."

"Then what's Jamie?"

"That remains to be seen."

"I think he's the one," Trish said sweetly.

Marissa studied her salad as she chopped at it with her knife and fork. Her breath had caught in her throat and was hung up there like an oversize leaf of escarole.

"Wait a minute." Sylvie angled her head low, trying to see Marissa's eyes. "It seems to me that if you're already having doubts—"

"I'm not!"

"Yes, you are."

Marissa shook her head. "If I am, they're doubts about me, not Jamie. I'm the one with faulty judgment. He's been—" She found her breath, a great gust of it. "He's everything I should want. Everything."

"There you go," Cass said after a moment of respectful silence. They recognized sincerity when they saw it.

Marissa set aside her misgivings. And her mood. "I haven't even told you about yesterday. I didn't go into work after all. Jamie was with me for most of the day, setting my house to straights—well, sort of. He got new locks. The apartment's barricaded like Fort Knox. And he went with me to the local precinct—"

Sylvie interrupted. "I thought you were going to the morgue."

Trish's mouth opened. "The morgue? You didn't tell me that!"

Marissa explained. "They found my intruder. Dead."

Trish shivered. Sylvie sliced a piece of steak. "You were able to identify him, then?"

"No. I went to the police station and they showed me a creepy Polaroid close-up of his face on a slab." Marissa's stomach revolted at the memory and she had to swallow hard. The only dead people she'd seen had been those at funerals, done up in makeup and their Sunday best. Death in the raw had shocked her, especially when she remembered that it might have been *her* being tagged and photographed. "Since the burglar wore a ski mask when he was in my apartment, I couldn't help. Still, they're pretty sure it's him. The ski mask was left beside his body, and he had a number of cavities, the way I said he did."

"Was there an ID on him?"

"His name was Freddy Bascomb." Marissa lifted her shoulders. "Which means nothing to me. The cops are looking into his background, to see if they can find any connection to explain what he wanted. Apparently this guy was just a common punk. I got the feeling that the cops will mark him as just another street thug and give the case low priority."

"But he was murdered," Trish protested.

Cassandra leaned her chin on her hand. "And by whom?"

"The other guy," Sylvie guessed. "The one you saw at the bottom of the fire escape."

"You have a criminal mind," Marissa said. "That's exactly what the cops suggested. A falling-out among thieves. Which only makes sense if they took something so valuable from me that it was worth killing over, and they didn't."

"But you don't know what they were after, so who's to say?"

Trish chimed in. "Maybe your break-in was only one of a string, and then they argued after yours went bad."

"Could be."

"I'll run the case by Sam," Cass volunteered. "See what he thinks."

"What does Jamie say?" Trish asked.

Marissa's lips puckered. "Oh, Jamie. He's more concerned with keeping me safe, but he did have a cockeyed theory about Shandi being involved."

Cass and Sylvie exchanged looks.

"Who's Shandi?" Trish had never met her.

"Shandi Lee. An old roommate of mine. She also dated Jamie for a very short time, years ago," Marissa said. "Anyway, Shandi's no longer a problem. I haven't seen her since—" She cut off abruptly.

Cass raised her brows. "The night of the break-in."

"Coincidence," Marissa insisted. "Shandi disappears when she finds a new guy or a new interest."

"Then why does Jamie suspect her?"

"We were only throwing out theories. I suppose it's because she's usually broke, but that's nothing new."

Marissa felt uncomfortable. There was something going on concerning Shandi, something that Jamie knew and she didn't. Not a dynamic she was used to. "Forget I brought it up. I don't want Shandi hearing about this."

"Maybe you're on the hit list of the jewel thief that Sam's after," Cass said to lighten up the mood. "Your law firm has sent you to a few fancy parties. It's possible."

"Uh-huh. Little Mari, Queen of the *Calle Oche* Low-riders, running around with a stash of jewels? Any thief worth his salt would know that my jewelry is all costume."

"You have those diamond solitaire earrings."

Marissa had bought them for herself as a special indulgence after her biggest case to date. She'd played a vital part in negotiating a good settlement for one of the firm's top clients. Afterward, Thomas Howard, the most senior of the senior partners, had begun greeting her by name and including her among the select group of favored associates. He'd even taken a fatherly interest in her, asking about her background and her ambitions for the future. Some said he was grooming her.

"And a pearl necklace," continued Cass. A gift from a devoted swain who'd clung to Marissa like an oyster.

"I still have them. The burglar didn't take a thing even after he busted through my bedroom door. But quarter-carat diamonds and one string of pearls hardly constitute a trove worthy of raiding."

"Cass, is this Sam of yours on the Zoey Zander case?" Trish asked. "I read about the heist in the paper."

"I was discussing that with my sister only last weekend," Cass said excitedly. "I went up to Fairfield, and we were sorting through the store of antiques in the basement of her shop. Morgan came across an old French text. She was able to translate a few words here and there—enough to realize that the book was telling the story of the same amulet that was among the items missing from the auction house."

"It's called the White Star." Trish dabbed her lips with a napkin. "I read about the amulet's history when I minored in art history at Northwestern."

"What's the legend?" Marissa asked.

"Hard to say." Cass tucked a strand of hair behind her ear. "Morgan's French was too limited. Trish?"

"I don't recall the details, except that the tale was supposed to be a thousand years old and it involved a legacy of true love." Trish shrugged. "My brother, Alex, is the one to ask. He does PR for the Museum of Antiquities. He would know who could help you."

Sylvie had finished her lunch and was growing impatient with talk of ancient legends and dusty tomes. "What does it look like?"

"There was a grainy photo of it in the Sunday *Times*," Cass said. "It's an ivory star."

Sylvie sniffed. "I'd rather have a platinum Rolex."

Marissa shooed her. "Your soul has no romance!"

"Not true. It's tucked into my lingerie drawer. I only take it out for special occasions."

"Sounds about right," Cass said drolly, and they were laughing again.

A longing, almost a craving, lingered within Marissa. Considering her recent turn in affection for Jamie, a prophecy of true love that was meant to be would certainly simplify her love life.

ALLARD WATCHED from a corner table as the four women got ready to leave the bistro. They didn't give him a glance. He had put on a suit and blended in with the crowd, remaining watchful and still except for the cell phone he'd lifted to his ear in imitation of the businessmen all around.

He'd been seated close enough to hear everything. He'd picked up a few interesting tips, verifying what he'd already deduced—though the blond "roommate" was no longer in the picture, the boyfriend on the fifth floor definitely was.

When they'd begun talking about the amulet, Allard's neutral expression had almost cracked. He was sweating from every pore before their words had sunk in and he'd realized that the women knew very little. For once, Lady Luck was on his side, Marissa still had no idea what she possessed.

While that confirmation had pleased him, he could not let down his guard. Not yet.

"But soon," he said into the dead telephone while he watched Marissa through the window. The women kissed cheeks, making their goodbyes. "Very soon."

Despite the pressure being applied by his employer, he'd taken his time planning the next recovery attempt. The days of surveillance and discreet inquiries were about to pay off.

Allard tossed aside the cell phone. He signaled the

waiter for the check. Marissa was hailing a cab, but there was no need to follow her back to work. He had a more lucrative destination in mind.

The Village. Marissa's brownstone.

But not her apartment, with its new locks and bolts. Oh, no.

Twenty minutes later, he was at the brownstone, on time for his appointment to view an apartment. The super buzzed him in. When Allard heard the man clumping upstairs from the basement, keys jingling, he stepped behind the door.

The super walked by, looking in vain for the apartment hunter who'd called and offered a large cash payment as key money. Allard disappeared into the gloom of a sublevel maintenance room, where the super spent most of his day behind a battered steel desk, eating doughnuts and gambling online.

The passkeys for all the apartments were hung on a labeled pegboard. Allard liberated the keys to 3C and made a quick wax impression. As the super's footsteps descended from above, he returned the keys, pocketed the small tin of wax and stepped deeper into the labyrinthine basement.

The darkness enfolded him.

He closed his eyes, listening for the super's grumbling complaints about being stood up. The desk chair squeaked. A TV clicked on, tuned to a horse race.

Allard waited for the man to become absorbed. Then he silently slipped past, smug with how easy it was to acquire a copy of Marissa Suarez's brand new keys.

9

THE OFFICES OF HOWARD, Coffman, Ellis and Schnitzer were situated in a glass-and-steel skyscraper in lower Manhattan. From Marissa's first day of employment, she'd felt powerful and cosmopolitan, tapping through the travertine lobby in her designer shoes and cunningly tailored power suits. She had held that potential image of herself while waitressing her way through college, during late-night cram sessions at Columbia Law, even the first time she'd swallowed her intimidation and walked through the door of a fashionable clothing store on Madison Avenue.

She'd believed that once she was that woman, her life would be complete.

And it was. If she didn't count her persistently unwise love life. But then, she'd never been the kind of woman who thought having a man was what would make her fulfilled, so it didn't count. Much.

Until recently, when she'd realized that it wasn't about finding "a man."

It was falling in love with *the* man.

I'm not in love, she thought. *What's going on is some*

strange symbiosis of danger, adrenaline, lust and famil-
iarity. I might be off my head, but I'm not in love.

Except there was the way she and Jamie had clicked.

That tiny little *click* that kept her up at night so she
couldn't even sleep in her own bed. Though she'd told
herself not to get too cozy, she'd ended up spending
most of the weekend with Jamie, at his place. He
thought that was because she was scared. Which she
was, but not of burglars.

Being scared wasn't easy for her to admit, not since
she was thirteen and her brothers had dared her to climb
to the top of a ghostly abandoned construction site in
their neighborhood. Saying "I can't" was worse to her
than anything else.

Nearing the elevators, Marissa slowed. She switched
her brief-bag to the other hand and smoothed her
charcoal pin-striped skirt, conservative except for the
slit in the back. That morning, she'd needed the extra
boost of confidence she got from being an attractive
woman who could make men beg at the sight of the back
of her knee.

Her nape was prickling.

She whirled around, half expecting to see Paul's big
toothpaste grin, the one he thought was so charming, but
there was no one except suits gathering to ride the
elevator. A security guard circled the lobby, stopping to
chat to the woman who ran the kiosk where Marissa
often picked up a *café con leche* on her way in.

She rubbed beneath her collar. Was the burglary still
making her jumpy? She should be over that by now.

She'd once kneed a man in the balls when he tried to feel her up on the subway, and had then reported to the courthouse to second chair a defendant's trial without a hair turned.

A movement caught her eye. A dark-haired man was slipping out the revolving door. No one she recognized, despite the tingling at her neck. She boarded the elevator.

On the twenty-fourth floor, she was greeted by the perky receptionist who sat behind a monolithic desk of burled walnut and ebony wood. Marissa moved quickly to her office, feeling as if she were running a gauntlet. She'd have to face Paul soon. After her coffee would be preferable.

She sent no-nonsense smiles and quick nods at those who greeted her. As usual, the mood at the law firm was subdued and serious. The code of behavior and dress was conservative. Marissa had seen Bill Schnitzer frowning at her skirts beneath his bristly walrus mustache.

As an up-and-comer, Marissa's office was a nice one. She had a window, a recent reward that had seemed momentous at the time. Her work life was more successful than her private life, but the thing about such achievements was that as soon as she'd accomplished one, she was on to the next. There was never an end. She never felt as satisfied or relaxed as she did hanging out with Jamie.

Her assistant, Ophelia Jackson, was waiting at her desk with a stack of messages, the open appointment book and a Tootsie Roll pop sticking out of the corner of her mouth. She was trying to quit smoking.

"Hey, O, didn't your dentist tell you sugar's bad for the teeth?" Marissa thought of the rotting breath of the burglar and suppressed a shiver.

"I should chew vitamins to stem my cravings? Not going to happen, honey." Ophelia was a forty-ish black woman of rounded proportions and a sassy attitude. She and Marissa shared an interest in fashion and a dedication to rising through the ranks.

Ophelia looked Marissa over. "Nice shoes, but didn't I tell you to wear a miniskirt so Paul will recognize what he lost when he decided to play beach-blanket bingo on ya?"

Marissa flashed the slit.

Ophelia's eyes widened. "Ooh. Subtle. I like it."

Marissa swung past the desk to her office door, snatching up the messages as she reached for the knob. "I'm going to play this off as discreetly as possible. For now, don't put through any calls from—"

She stopped in the doorway. "Paul."

He lounged in her chair with his feet up on her desk, smiling as if nothing had happened between them. Ophelia appeared at Marissa's shoulder, making apologies. "He's been waiting for fifteen minutes. I can get rid of him if you'll let me use the staple remover."

"It'll be fine." *I hope.* Marissa dumped her bag on one of the empty visitor's chairs. "Maybe next time."

Ophelia crossed her arms, frowning at Paul. "I don't like him thinking he can get past me any old time. Truth is, I never even tried."

Marissa loomed over him, hands on hips. "And I appreciate that, O. If there's a next time, you have my okay to use any means necessary to keep him out."

Paul looked from one peeved woman to the other, then removed his feet from the desk, laughing a bit nervously. "Hey, ladies. Why so touchy? What happens in the Caymans, stays in the Caymans." He stood and tried to put his arms around Marissa.

She evaded. "Don't bother."

"I was hoping you'd have cooled off by now. But you're still the same hot tamale, aren't you?" He actually thought the canard was a compliment.

"Yes, and I'm an angry black woman." Ophelia rolled her eyes at Marissa. Her expression said, *I never knew what you saw in this yahoo.*

Neither did Marissa, although the evidence was in front of her eyes. There was no denying that Paul was a handsome devil, with ice-blue eyes and short dark hair combed over his forehead in a careful wave. He was smart, yet deceptively shallow. Before she'd heard his recycled banter a hundred times, he'd seemed mildly amusing.

He was all flash, no substance. Even as a girl, she'd been attracted to shiny objects, such as the glitzy jewelry at the carnival that turned her skin green. She hadn't learned her lesson then, either, spending all her piggy-bank savings on games of chance before she'd learned that she couldn't afford foolish risks.

Paul shot the cuffs of his pin-striped shirt. "We have to talk."

"We talked. I have no more to say."

"Then you can listen."

Marissa shooed her hand at him. "Not now. I have work to catch up on."

Pointedly, Ophelia held the door open.

Paul ignored her. "I'll talk in front of her if I have to."

Ophelia snorted at the "her."

Marissa sat and paged through the messages. She was trying not to look at Paul and especially Ophelia, who was making faces behind his back. "O won't mind."

Paul dropped heavily into the chair opposite her desk. "You're so cold."

"Two seconds ago, I was a hot tamale."

"Don't be that way, Marissa."

Her hackles rose. He'd used an intimate tone, a throatiness that she used to think was sexy. Maybe still did. She was mad that he continued to have an effect on her, involuntary and unwanted though it was.

"Let's get this over with then." She looked at Ophelia, who shrugged and stepped out of the office, closing the door with a quiet *click.*

Marissa inhaled. There had been no *click* with Paul. Only the easy glide of slipping in and out of a relationship that had never gone beyond the superficial during the two months they'd seen each other.

"I'm sorry," Paul said, startling her. "I shouldn't have neglected you on the vacation. I thought you'd understand about work—that was why the firm bought our tickets."

"You didn't tell me the firm was paying our way!"

"Does it matter?"

"Obviously not to you." Furious now, she picked up the current files Ophelia had left on the desk and tapped them against the hard surface, aligning the edges. There was something to be said for order. Neat, clean, efficient. Why couldn't she have that clarity in every part of her life?

She thought of Sunday morning with Jamie, snuggled in his lumpy sofa bed with the linens atangle and the newspaper in pieces, spread all around. Tufts of dog hair had collected in the corners. The leash hung off the doorknob. His running shoes sat in the middle of the floor, with the sweatpants that trailed one inside-out leg because he'd stepped out of them when she'd opened the blanket to reveal her nudity.

Her temperature rose. Cleanliness was *not* next to sexiness.

She looked up and Paul's smile was almost gloating. "I can see you want me back."

"Get your eyes checked."

"This is it, you know. Last chance." His cleft chin rose high above his collar. "I don't grovel for any woman."

But he'd come close to it. Not really for her, she thought, unsure of what his true motive had been. "Fine, then," she said. "Tell me this conversation is as over as the relationship."

"What about—"

"I don't care what happened on the beach. We were through even before that."

"Then you *don't* have pictures?"

Understanding washed over her. "Is that what all of this has been about? You thought I'd pass photos of you and your bimbo around the office, maybe cost you a partnership?"

Paul was expressionless. His knuckles were white.

"I'm not vindictive. I only want this to be over." She waved at him. "Go on. Get out of here. There are no photos."

"You said there were."

She grinned wryly. "I was being vindictive."

Paul seemed relieved as he got up. He shook the tension out of his shoulders, tugged his tie into place. "So we're through. Too bad. You're the best looking chick at this firm. We could have made a damn fine team. A power couple."

Mr. and Mrs. Shark. She wasn't even remotely interested.

"I'll see you around." Marissa calmly opened her first file, trying not to show her triumph. She was pleased that he'd given up so easily, if a bit suspicious. "Watch out for Ophelia on the way out. She bites."

SKIP SISMAN TRUNDLED his heavy frame into the staff break room at the *Village Observer.* "Whatcha got for me?" he asked Jamie, having caught sight of him on the way back from lunch. Sisman looked lost without a pastry, like a teenager without an MP3 player. He did have a spot of mustard—or custard—on his tie.

Jamie put an oversize mug of water into the microwave. "You're not still after me about doing your research, are you? I won't. And I thought the story was dead anyway." The paper had run only the obligatory "the case remains open" follow-up.

"Nothing much happening." Sisman huffed. "That's why we got to lean on the human interest angle."

"*We* aren't leaning on anything but the countertop. I've got other work to do."

"So help me out with the basics. I can massage them into a story."

"I don't embellish facts."

Sisman flexed his sausage fingers. "I said *massage, man.*"

The microwave beeped. Jamie rummaged through the cupboard for dried soup mix. "What's it matter to you? Aunt Dena's not coming through with the goods?"

"I told you, nothing's happening. You'd think a few of the pieces would have been fenced or pawned by now, right? But I got zilch."

Jamie shook the empty box. Raided again. He flattened the carton and made a rebound shot into the waste can. "What about the suspects?"

Sisman hitched up his belt. "Info's dried up."

"No impending arrests?"

"Aunt—the cops figure the thief's lying low."

Jamie took the hot water from the microwave and popped in a little tub of macaroni and cheese labeled in Magic Marker: Alice S. Do Not Eat!!!

As soon as the timer beeped, he grabbed the food and a plastic fork. "Good luck with your story."

"I'm running down a list of possible prime suspects,"

Sisman called after him, "but you gotta help. You're the culture guy!"

"Sorry. I have my own stuff that I've been avoiding." The *Guys and Dolls* passes remained unused.

Jamie worked his way back to his desk, forking up the cheesy noodles. Tasted like home, when he'd foraged the cupboards on school-day afternoons. Marissa would scowl. She despised processed food.

He picked up the phone to call her, then put it down. Not a good idea to interrupt Marissa when she was in work mode, even for the scoop on the return of Paul Beckwith. He didn't know why he was concerned. There was no doubt in his mind that she was through with Paul.

So it had to be the same old doubt—that *he* would go the way of Paul and all the other exes.

The fork snapped between his fingers. He tossed it away, muttering, "For chrissake. Quit being such a girl."

Enough was enough. He was out of patience.

Marissa responded to challenges. From now on, instead of taking it easy, he was taking charge. If he had to, he'd *make* her love him.

How to do that was anyone's guess.

"WORK GO OKAY, babe?"

Marissa had returned to the kitchen after letting Jamie in through the Fort Knox barricade. "Don't you mean, how was the encounter with Paul?"

Jamie halted in the doorway. "Did you see him?"

"He was waiting in my office when I got there."

"Oh." Jamie dumped a plastic bag of ginger root onto

the counter. He'd picked it up on the way home, at her request. Taking charge didn't have to preclude all domestic responsibilities.

Marissa was cooking. With her long hours, she didn't often take the time to prepare meals during the week. But she'd told him of her fond memories of being in the kitchen with her mother and sister, singing pop songs while they chopped and mixed and fried. Apparently there was a lot of chopping and mixing and frying to be done for a family of six with many intrusive but endearing relatives.

While his own family had lacked some of that togetherness, he'd had enough of a taste that he liked to think how he and Marissa could make their own traditions. Sunday dinners in a city apartment. Just the two of them. Or maybe family time, when there were children.

Shit. He was going girly again. Turning into the kind of sentimental fool that Marissa disdained.

"Paul's nothing to be bothered with.". She picked up a bunch of cilantro, slapped the leafy herb on the cutting board and ran the knife through it. "It was the same story as when he called from the islands. He pretended to want me back, but all he really cared about was covering his ass with the partners."

Jamie dipped a finger into a lime puree. "Are you sure he won't make trouble for you?"

"That's always a possibility. But he'd be a fool to fuss when that would reflect on him, too. He has to know I wouldn't go down without a fight."

She sounded brave, but he could tell that she was

worried. The partners were a conservative bunch and the competition for promotion was rabid. A messy office romance would be a giant black mark on their records.

Jamie touched her elbow. "It'll be okay. You're a killer. The partners love you."

"Killer," she repeated doubtfully.

He found that interesting. A week ago she'd have relished the description.

Marissa slammed the knife on a clove of garlic. "I'm not going soft!"

"Of course not." So he wasn't the only one?

"Sorry. Thinking out loud." She cleared her throat. "Speaking of the partners, I have a command performance with them this week. A dinner party at Mr. Coffman's house on Friday. Only a few of the associates were invited."

"Will Paul be there?"

"I'm sure. But stop worrying about him. He's inconsequential."

"I'm not worried. It's just that…" Jamie gave up with a shake of his head, then had to brush back his hair. His doubts remained about Paul, but he intended to take care of them his own way.

"You need a haircut." She'd always admired the way his long dark lashes framed his bedroom eyes. "But I like you this way. Kind of shaggy and unkempt. Makes me feel better about my imperfections."

"You have imperfections?"

"You're asking that of a woman who serially dates Mr. Wrong and keeps two years of fashion magazines stacked in the fireplace?" She looked around for something else to chop up for the ceviche, but she was finished. "About the dinner party."

"Yes?"

"Want to come?"

"Who, me?"

"Don't be a dork."

"I'd better get a haircut."

She ruffled his already-ruffled hair. "You're handsome the way you are."

"Tell you what, I'll go if you'll come with me to a play I have to review. It's off-off Broadway, a kooky revival of *Guys and Dolls*. We can go to the Saturday matinee so our evening isn't ruined."

"That's a fine way for an objective critic to talk."

He smiled sheepishly.

"It's a deal," she said.

Jamie ran upstairs to take Sally out. He came back in jeans and they finished making dinner.

When they were ready to eat, he uncorked the wine, she cleared the table of junk mail, proud of herself when she tipped three-fourths of it into the trash can. Her good plates came out, colorful Fiestaware, with goblets for the wine and woven reed place mats.

Jamie entered the small dining area with the wine bottle in one hand and a dish of olives in the other. When he reached to kiss her, his lips stretched open and she saw he held an olive between his teeth. She bit into it and they chewed and swallowed and kissed and laughed.

They were still at the table, lingering over the last

bites of the yellow fin ceviche, when a sound at the door made Jamie leap out of his chair.

"Who is it?" he barked.

A key slid into the lock. The knob wiggled back and forth. "Hey, what's with the door?"

"It's Shandi." Marissa looked down at the bread knife in her hand. She dropped it onto the cutting board. "This is ridiculous. I'm jumpier than Harry."

Jamie let Shandi in. "Some people knock first."

"Sure, cutie." She barged past him, wearing a gaping sleeveless basketball jersey over a tube top and jean shorts. Her hair was standing on end, scooped off her face by a bandanna, and there was a new hole in her ear, stuck through with a dangling skeleton key that dragged down her lobe. "I came by to pick up my things." She plucked an olive from the dish. "Hiya, Mari. You changed the locks? Should I take that personally?"

"There was a break-in."

"That sucks." Shandi sat. "Can I have this?" she asked, taking the platter of tuna. She shoveled a bite into her mouth with her fingers. "What is it, sushi? Did they nip my stuff?"

"Nothing was stolen."

"Cool."

"What happened to you?" Jamie asked. "Where've you been?"

"Here and there." She shrugged. "Out and about. Uptown and down low."

"There was a *break-in,* Shandi," Marissa said, leaning forward over the table. "I was assaulted."

Shandi stopped chewing. "You mean—"

"I came home, the thief was still here and grabbed me, but I got away."

"Did you tell anyone the apartment had been empty?" Jamie demanded.

Shandi frowned. "I don't think so, but…" She shrugged. "I say a lot of things to a lot of people."

"What about Marissa's belongings? Did you 'borrow' something of hers? Maybe something she brought back from vacation?"

"Nope." Shandi ran a tongue over her teeth. "Who put you in charge? Am I under arrest or what?"

"No, of course not," Marissa said. "It's just that there have been some strange happenings around here lately, and we thought you might be able to help."

"Do you know a man named Freddy Bascomb?" Jamie asked.

Shandi dropped a butter knife. "Sorry," she muttered.

"Well?"

"No."

"You're sure?"

"As sure as I can be." Shandi left the table, reappearing a minute later with her bags and makeup case. A battered Prada backpack hung off one arm. "Hey, you guys, this is really interesting and all that, but I've got to go."

"Why so fast?" Jamie said, Mr. Sarcastic.

"Let her leave." Marissa went to the door with Shandi. "You know you could tell me if you're mixed up in a bad situation, right?"

Shandi looked away for a moment, then reverted to her usual self as she showily crossed her chest and raised her hand. "I swear I didn't have anything to do with the break-in."

Marissa gave her a quick hug. "I believe you." But there was a remaining doubt.

Shandi clutched briefly, then pulled away. "It's good to see you and Jamie together. Stick with him. He's lots better for you than…the other guys."

"Do you mean Paul?"

"Maybe." Shandi's smile didn't reach her eyes. "I'm sorry I'm such a lousy friend." She dropped Marissa's old key into her hand, no longer bothering with the fake smile. "Watch your back."

"What does that mean?" Marissa's scalp prickled. "Wait. Do you have an address? A number?"

"If you want me, call my cell." Shandi waved as she disappeared down the stairs.

Marissa shut the door. Jamie stood nearby, watching. "You were rude," she said. "I don't know if I've ever seen you be rude before."

"She caught me by surprise. I didn't mean to chase her out. I had more questions to ask her."

"Don't take this 'being my protector' thing too far, okay? I can deal with some *machismo*—God knows I'm used to it with my dad and brothers—but there's a limit."

Jamie fisted his hands; the sinew and muscle in his arms flexed and tightened. Suddenly she was taken with what a nice physique he'd developed. She knew, of course she knew, but now that they were lovers she was free to really revel in the attraction. She'd been suppressing a lot of sexual hunger.

"Sorry," he said, "but I'm not stepping back. As long as you're in danger, your business is my business."

What she got was another of the distracting thrills. Not very liberated of her, especially when she usually found male bossiness very grating. She couldn't even get prickly about taking care of herself. There was something deeply comforting about having a strong man in her corner, protecting her *and* encouraging her. "I've been perfectly safe for the past several days."

"Because you've been at my place."

She thought it was best to change the subject. "Did you hear what Shandi said about being a bad friend? And watching my back?"

Jamie nodded, suddenly wary.

"Does that make any kind of sense to you?" Marissa tensed. "I'm guessing it does." She walked toward him, staring hard into his eyes so he wouldn't look away. She poked a finger into his chest. "I want you to tell me without pulling any punches."

"I don't want to be the one—"

"*Tell* me."

He blew out a breath. "All right. A couple of months ago, not long after you'd started dating Paul, I saw him in a bar on Prince Street. You know it. Macintosh's. My kind of place, not his. It was midnight and I was there because—well, whatever. But it was late."

"Why were you there? Were you drunk?"

"That doesn't matter."

"Tell me. I want the whole story."

Jamie turned away, his head hunched between his shoulders. "You were going out with Paul that night, and you'd told me you two were getting serious. I thought it might be *the* night. You know what I mean." He checked her reaction. "I didn't feel like sitting at home, thinking about what you were doing with Paul, so I went to Mac's to drown my sorrows. Okay?"

Regret welled up inside her. "I didn't know you were feeling that way. I am so sorry."

"Yeah." He tilted his head back, his Adam's apple moving in his throat. "Anyway, I guess it wasn't the night after all, because suddenly there was Paul, stopping by for a drink after your date."

"He didn't see you?"

"I made sure of that. I wasn't in the mood."

"So what happened?"

"Shandi came in."

"Oh. I see."

"After a while, they, uh…"

She knew he was trying to spare her feelings by not describing the events, but she could guess what he'd left out. Shandi was a flirt. Paul was a ladies' man. One plus one equals two rotten louses.

Jamie's brows knitted. He had to force his voice out. "They left together."

"You're sure it was—?" She saw the look on his face and suddenly found herself laughing and shaking her head and gulping at air. "Of course it was. Of course."

Reckless energy boiled up in her. She didn't blame

Jamie, not a bit. But she needed a release. When he made a motion toward her, she shoved him away. "Why didn't you tell me?"

"How could I?"

Constricted by the walls around her, she walked in an agitated little circle, waving her arms. "How could you *not?* I would have never continued seeing Paul."

"Are you sure of that?" Jamie asked quietly. Always the calm center of her tornado. "Or would you have decided that I was interfering because I was jealous over you?"

"I've always trusted you."

"Yes, but you know how it goes. Kill the messenger. Our friendship might have been ruined. As much as I hated it, I had to let you find out for yourself."

"You let me get burned."

His face was harsh with the consequences of that decision. "I tried to warn you. I even tried to get Shandi to confess, but she claimed I'd gotten it wrong. She'd turned Paul down."

"Could that be true?"

"You decide."

Drained, Marissa went to sit on the couch. Jamie hovered nearby. She gestured at him. "Go home. I need to be alone now so I can get my head straight." She was a smart woman. Why had she willfully disregarded the signs that Paul wasn't worthy of her? Simply to make it easier to get out of the relationship?

Jamie plopped himself opposite her. "I'm not leaving."

She glared.

He settled deeper. "You're stuck with me, through thick and thin."

There'd be no budging him. She was miffed, yes, but also grateful somewhere beneath the hurt and confusion. She thought of her parents, who fought and loved with equal passion.

Funny how for years she'd believed that she wanted to stay far away from their sort of marriage. And now, with Jamie, she was beginning to understand what true love meant.

Sticking with each other, through thick and thin. Good and bad. Love and lies.

10

"COME SNUGGLE with me, babe."

Marissa waited a beat. "You talkin' to me or the dog?"

Jamie patted the bed. "Who do you think?"

"The dog," she said when Sally rose from her scroungy cushion in the corner of the pocket-size kitchen and padded across the room to lay her head near Jamie's hand.

He looked at Marissa over the top of his wire-framed reading glasses. "Jealous?"

"As if. Blondes do *not* have more fun." She tapped a folded-over page of the *Village Observer* with an ink pen. She was in a tank top and a pair of his pajama bottoms, curled up in his reading chair with the crossword. "Besides, I have Harry. If he'd just come down from the bookshelf."

They were holed up in Jamie's small apartment again. Despite the new locks and bars, he could see that Marissa still wasn't comfortable at her own place. She wouldn't admit it, so he'd claimed that Sally couldn't sleep in a strange place and he didn't want to leave her alone.

Neither of them had suggested that they might sleep apart, even though there'd been several awkward moments when one or the other had started to comment on their change in situation, only to back off when the magnitude became apparent. He spent his time trying not to think that Marissa had turned to him only in a time of need and that before long she would be back up on her high heels, mowing down the opposition with a wink and a toss of her ponytail.

He had no idea what she thought. She wasn't talking, except for muffled telephone conversations with Cass that turned to fake blather about sample sales when he walked into the room.

If not for that worry, plus the break-in, the body in the morgue, the Paul and Shandi problems, and the fact that Marissa hadn't uttered a word of promising affection, Jamie would have believed he was living a dream. He was finally with her. That should have been enough.

"C'mere," he crooned, scratching Sally's muzzle.

"I'm finishing the crossword."

He propped his open book on his chest. "Let me help." The faster she was done, the sooner he'd have her in bed beside him.

She gave him a look before perusing the empty squares. "Replica. Six spaces. Last letter *Y*."

"Easy. Effigy."

"Not bad." Her eyes narrowed and he knew she was searching for a stumper. "Portent. Six spaces."

"No letters?"

"Nope." Her pen tapped impatiently.

"Oh, the pressure." He folded his arms behind his head. Sally looked at him with disappointed eyebrows, then retreated to her dog bed. "How about augury?"

A short pause while Marissa examined the squares. "That works."

"Are you done yet?"

"Why so impatient?"

He took his book, stuck a marker where he'd left off, and laid it on the end table with his glasses and his alarm clock and the box of condoms that would soon need replacing. Hot damn.

"We're still in the honeymoon period," he said, flipping back the blanket. *Honeymooners without a future.* "Let's enjoy it."

Marissa chewed on the end of her pen, contemplating him with mischief dancing in her eyes. "Four-word phrase. Eleven letters."

He counted on his fingers. "How about—no, that's three words."

"First letter *S*," she said. "Last letter *E*."

There were too many possibilities. "Suck my—"

"No profanity allowed!" She was laughing.

So was he, relieved that they still had a semblance of their previous rapport. "You have to give me a clue."

"What you should have said instead of 'Come snuggle with me.'"

Knowing Marissa, she'd be blunt. "Stick it to me," he guessed.

"That's terrible." She put her feet down and tossed the paper on the coffee table he'd shoved out of the way to make room for the open sofa bed. "But you're heading in the right direction." She stood and stretched. Her breasts lifted beneath the skimpy top, pert nipples making pinpoints for his gaze. "C'mon, Mr. Puzzle Man."

"Seduce me..." He was at a loss.

"Did I stump you?"

"Uh." He'd erected a pup tent in his boxer shorts.

She saw. "So *stump* is the wrong word."

"Thanks for the compliment."

Her hands were on her hips, the pajama bottoms riding low. Her hip bones were prominent and her belly was flat, the color of heavy cream, accented by the glint of gold at her pierced navel. He scooted higher on the bed, his hard-on burgeoning. She didn't have to act sexy. Simply her presence was enough to turn him on, even when there was no promise of more than physical gratification.

"'Save me, Jamie,'" he guessed.

"That doesn't fit the clue, and it's only three words." She rolled her eyes. "Not very empowering, either."

"Then you can save me."

"You got it." She pounced onto the bed, crawling over him on her hands and knees. Her mouth dipped to kiss and nibble across his face. "Sex me up, babe," she whispered, breathing hotly in his ear.

He put his hands on her luscious ass. "Is that it? The magic words?"

"Not romantic enough for you?"

Her hair was long and loose, falling in his face. Freshly scented with the strawberry shampoo she'd brought up from her place. He brushed his fingers through it, cradling her face. "Not romantic enough for *you*."

"I don't need—" She stopped, closed her eyes. He knew what she'd intended to say. "Maybe I do."

His hopes leaped. "Four words," he said, kissing her softly, quickly. "Starts with *I*. Ends with *Marissa*."

She bumped him with her forehead. Pressed her fingers over his mouth. "Shh."

"I can't," he said. *Stupid, stupid.* He'd been trying to play this out, stay cool, keep his heart off his sleeve, but it was no use. He had to be himself, not the men that she'd dated—and dumped. "I love you, Marissa."

She rolled off him. Her face dropped into the pillow. "You had to go and say it."

His expectations plummeted. "You had to already know how I felt."

"Yeah, but saying it out loud is different." She made a muffled screeching sound that quit abruptly, as if she'd bit a chunk out of the pillow.

When she looked up, her face was pink, her eyes pulled into narrow slits. "You know I love you, too."

"But not in the same way."

"I love you as a friend, and I love—"

"This," he said, flipping over and pressing himself against her prone body. His erection hadn't wilted. In fact, he felt even more aroused, swollen with hot, angry pride, as if his cock could make her love him if he was hard enough and good enough. If he could make her come until she was swimming in the proof that her feelings were stronger than she'd admit.

"Aggh." She squirmed beneath him as he pushed the pajama bottoms down, baring her ass. "Slow down."

"I don't think so." Reaching beneath her, he found the tight bead of one nipple and tugged on it. "You can tell me to stop, and I will. But you won't do that. You want this too much."

She panted. "Yeah? You think?"

"I know." His knee parted her thighs. Her heat was apparent even before his hand slipped along the enticing curve of her bottom to the slickened folds that gave way to the press of his fingers. He wiggled them inside her and she clenched down, shuddering around the invasion.

"See?" he said, waving his fingers, showing her the shiny wetness. She moved her face away and he kissed and bit at her nape until finally she turned her head, watching him with one wild white-rimmed eye.

He put his fingers in his mouth and sucked, savoring the taste of her like a lollipop before slowly pulling them out from between his puckered lips. His nostrils flared. Her fragrance should be bottled as an aphrodisiac and sold in secret back alleys in exotic foreign countries.

Marissa was stunned. "Dammit, Jamie. What's gotten into you?"

She should be asking what had got out. Having her evade his declaration had freed his inner brute. "Like it?" he growled, squeezing the firm flesh of her butt as he ground against her. A raging lust boiled his bloodstream, swelling and stiffening him until he felt as if he could punch through a bulkhead metal door with his erection.

"Yes!" She bucked beneath him. "I like it."

"Get me a rubber."

Blindly, she slapped her hand on the box, spilling condoms as she dragged it across the bed. One rip and she'd torn open a packet and was flinging the rolled latex disk over her shoulder. "Here."

He lifted his hips to apply the protection.

Seeing his distraction, she tried to crawl out from beneath him. He gripped her between his thighs, every muscle he'd developed from biking and Frisbee flexing in concentrated effort.

Her hands spread, seeking leverage, but she flopped like a fish on the beach. "Let me go."

"No." He finished and pressed his full weight down on her. "You'll like this, I promise."

"The pets," she said, grasping at straws.

They were sleeping. "That excuse only works once."

"You're being mean."

"And nasty." He stroked both hands along her back, tracing the narrowing of her waist, the flare of her hips. He reached around. She gasped and lifted her butt higher off the bed. Tempting him, the minx.

He humped against her. A pleased murmur slipped past her lips before she buried her face in the pillow crumpled between her elbows. She laced her fingers at the back of her neck, bracing herself as he entered her.

He grunted. "Ah-hh."

She bit down on a moan. "You say the nicest things."

"I tried, but you don't need romance, right?"

"I said 'maybe.'"

"When you decide, let me know, but for now—I—

uh—" The impossibly tight clasp of her wet flesh was shorting out his brain. He plowed deeper, until his balls were bumping up against her. A small whimper broke free of the pillow, and then the tension in her shoulders let go and she became supple and bendy like a willow branch, swaying with the currents that coursed between them.

He used his hips. The slippery friction was maddeningly good. Eventually she flattened out and he lifted her up until she was able to get her legs beneath her. He rose to his knees, spreading his fingers across her slim, bowed back as she arched and twisted and gripped him in a velvet vise. How beautiful she was, how untamable.

She rocked backward to meet his next thrust and then they were off on a wild galloping ride, pounding toward climax. He closed his eyes, concentrating on the rhythm and the drive, his racing heart.

Marissa's body had tightened again, squeezing spasmodically. She was up on her hands and knees, flinging her head, gnashing her teeth. Her black hair churned. He reached for the tangled tresses, pressing his lips to her spine and feeling for her trembling shoulders as he jammed his cock deep within her. A powerful orgasm ripped through him in pulse after pulse.

Panting heavily, he lowered them both to the bed. She clawed at the sheets, still shaking beneath him. Her skin was damp with sweat, the heat at the center of her rising under his palms as he separated their bodies. She rolled, facing away from him.

The pajamas were a snarl around her ankles, effectively shackling her, but she didn't kick free. He laid back and admired her sweet heart-shaped ass, rosy from their thrashing consummation.

After a while, when their breathing had slowed, he traced a line along her hip. "You have a great body."

"Thanks."

"And you're really good in bed."

"You, too."

Damn, he couldn't stop touching her. "See how non-chalant I can be?"

"That's enough, Jamie." She threw an elbow. "I get it."

He yanked his hand away. "All right. I concede. I shouldn't have rushed the dreaded *L* word."

"No," she said, and his heart dropped, until she turned over and propped herself up to look at him. Her face was infused—confused—with emotion. She was struggling with her response, and he wished he really could be the white knight who'd resolve all her questions.

"You said what you needed to." She bit her lip. "I respect that."

He draped one arm around her. "I wanted you to know. Let's leave it at that." For the time being.

"Good grief, will you stop being so understanding!" She darted at him with her teeth bared. For a second he thought she was going to bite off his nose to spite herself, but she landed an openmouthed kiss on him instead. "You should want to wale on me."

He gave her a quirky smile. "Well, yeah. I already did that."

Her cheeks colored. She went sloe-eyed. "Mmm, yes. So you did."

He stroked her arm. "Are you sleepy?"

"No."

"So we can talk."

She made a face. "By now, you should know that I'm not a sweet nothings kind of girl."

"Tell me what kind you are, then."

"You know me as well as anyone."

"Not you as a young girl. I bet you were a cute little thing."

"Gack, no. I was skinny and scabby. Always fighting with my brothers and getting into scrapes."

"Yeah, that sounds right. But I still think you were a cute little thing. Remember, your mother showed me photos when they came to visit."

"And how mortifying was that?"

"I had a very good time." He'd taken her parents out to dinner and a show. Parents always loved him, sometimes more than their daughters. That hadn't pained him all that much till now.

"Sure you did," Marissa said. "My mom loved you because you're genuine and funny and my dad was almost giddy with relief because I had a man who'd protect me without having sex with me."

"Ha, guess I blew that."

"What *Papi* doesn't know…"

Jamie frowned. "But I want him to know. I want everyone to know." He wanted to literally shout it from the rooftops. He loved Marissa and she—

Was still thinking of him as a temporary port in the storm.

"Don't go there," she mumbled, leaning her cheek on his chest.

"Then tell me about the first time you had sex." He wanted to say *fell in love*. Bad idea.

She was silent. On the big round cushion, Sally whimpered and paddled her feet. "Chasing Frisbees," Jamie said.

Marissa's head cocked. "Do you know what a *quinceanera* is?"

"Something to do with fruit and sex?"

"Good guess." She twined their arms, locked their fingers. "But wrong, except in my case, perhaps. A *quince* party is a Cuban tradition, a debut of sorts on a girl's fifteenth birthday. The entry to womanhood." She kissed his knuckles. "I, unfortunately, took the meaning literally."

"What did you do?"

"Ditched the party early. We had it in our backyard, folding tables among the rose bushes and vegetable garden. There were strings of paper lanterns. Huge trays of black beans and rice, *papas rellanas* and *pastelitos*. Music by somebody's cousin's mariachi band. Cackling relatives and "uncles" who patted my ass when they weren't cheating at dominoes. I swiped a bottle of rum and ran off with the neighbor boy who was visiting from his first semester at Florida State."

"You have a thing for neighbor boys, huh?"

"Hmm, yes. This one was just old enough to seem cool and adult to a girl who couldn't wait to shake the dust of the barrio off her heels."

Behind his closed lids, Jamie saw her dancing, twirling, lifting her party skirt to flash long bare legs.

"We went to the beach to skinny-dip. Afterward, I jumped Jose in the sand, behind some rocks. I just wanted to do it—get it over with. But he must have learned his technique at drunken frat parties because the sex was bad. Really bad."

Now he saw her hugging herself on a rock-strewn beach, trying to look blasé about her disillusionment. "Damn," he said, reaching over to stroke her back. "Teenage boys don't know what they're doing."

"No big deal." She caught his hand and tucked it beneath her chin. "What about you? How was your first time?"

"Uh…"

"You probably studied up before you did it. Learned all the positions, memorized diagrams of female anatomy—"

He laughed. "No diagrams. I wasn't that big a dork."

"So how old were you?"

"This is embarrassing. Nineteen. My first real girl-friend, freshman year of college. We were both virgins, so if we did it badly we didn't know the difference."

"Really? I thought kids in suburbs do it like bunnies, breaking out the booze and weed, having wild orgies while their parents are at work."

"I was too shy. And clean. After my dad died, Mom was on her own and she took the job of raising us very seriously. She went to a drug prevention class and was vigilant about keeping an eye out for signs of bad behavior. She even checked the levels in the bottles of cough syrup and tubes of model-toy glue."

"My dad was worse."

"You were lucky to have him."

"I know. Lucky and cursed. But I shouldn't complain." She sighed. "Do you still miss your father?"

"It's been a long time. The memories have faded. It's not missing him as much as it is now and then running up against the realization that there'll always be a hole in my life."

In the Wilson family, Jamie was the youngest son, thirteen when his father had succumbed to cancer. With his older siblings at after-school jobs or extracurricular activities, he'd been charged with babysitting his sister, Amy, who was four years younger. They were still close. He'd taken Marissa to Amy's wedding only last year. He hadn't minded that everyone had presumed Marissa was his girlfriend. Since then, every time he talked to his mother, she asked after Marissa, hoping for an announcement even though he'd 'fessed up that they were only friends.

Only friends. He hated that phrase.

"You'll be a great dad," Marrisa said, with a catch in her voice.

"Yeah, I'm going to make some woman very happy."

He stopped and waited to see what she'd say about *that*.

She cleared her throat with a short cough. "Some woman, hm?"

He gave her a one-armed hug. "You're some kind of woman, Marissa Suarez." He kissed her hair. "You smell like strawberries," he said. "And sesame noodles." They'd ordered in.

"It's my new scent. Eau de takeout." She snuffled against his neck. "You smell like sex."

"Yeah, I'm a rutting beast."

"Pah. You're a sweetheart and I want you to know that I do love you." Her face was scrunched by the effort of grappling with her words. "I—I just don't know if I can promise to *love* love you. It's too—" she swallowed "—too soon for that."

"When will it be *not* too soon?"

"That's impossible to say."

"Okay. We'll let it ride."

She shook her head. "That's horrible for you. Sorry." Her head continued wagging back and forth. "Sorry, sorry, sorry."

"Don't feel too bad for me. I'll take my compensations in the meantime."

"I do have to go to work."

"Damn, so no keeping you barefoot and naked?"

She called up a slightly melancholy smile. "Meet you here for a lunchtime quickie."

Jamie's thoughts were going in another direction. "How's it been at work? Has Paul bothered you?"

"I reassured him that I had no intention of bringing our personal issues into the office." Marissa moved restlessly. "But he's still acting funny. Always watching me. Fortunately, we're not working together on any of our cases, so I can avoid him quite easily."

"Still, you're concerned."

"Well, yes. There's probably been executive washroom talk. But I'll get past it."

"Sure. You're a warrior. You can get past anything."

Jamie found little comfort for himself in that. Although it was nice having no worries that Marissa would be tempted to forgive Paul, he also had to acknowledge that when a relationship was over for her, it was over.

She saw black and white, good and bad, right and wrong.

And once she'd made up her mind about ending a relationship, she never looked back.

11

"I HOPE YOU'RE NOT expecting me to schmooze like a lawyer," Jamie whispered to Marissa as they stood at the top of the steps leading down to Bradley Coffman's spacious living room. A wall of windows overlooked a spectacular view of the city, sparkling on the clear spring evening like the diamonds at Mrs. Coffman's throat. The cocktail hour was in full swing. "I can't understand half of what you people talk about."

"Don't even try to follow the lawyerly gobbledygook," she advised. "Most of them have no other life to talk about. They'll be thrilled to hear about your job. The spouses, especially."

"Oh, I'm to be shunted off with the other wives?"

"That's sexist." She smirked. "In so many ways."

He tugged on the network of spaghetti straps crisscrossed over the almost backless rear view of her little black cocktail number. "Call me a chauvinist, but I can't wait to unlace you from this dress."

She wiggled her shoulders. "Be good."

"You like me better when I'm bad."

He was teasing. Yet there was also a lot of truth in

the statement. She seemed to get especially passionate when other emotions spilled over into the lovemaking. But only allowable emotions. They were stuck at *Go*. A nice place to linger, but not to build a life on.

Marissa nudged Jamie. "Talk about bad. There he is."

Paul Beckwith looked debonair in one of his sharp suits with a silver tie. Jamie had unearthed his suit from the back of the closet and promised Marissa sexual favors if she'd iron out the wrinkles.

He made a low sound in his throat, watching Paul circulate like a shark. Licensed to schmooze.

"Just stay away from him, okay?" Marissa asked. "I can't have trouble at this party. Not even a raised voice."

"Fine. But you stay away, too."

"That should be easy. I've been avoiding him in the office all week." She hitched up her shoulders. "Into the fray."

Jamie took her hand as they walked down the steps into the party. There were about sixteen guests. Avoiding Paul entirely might not be possible. Too bad. Jamie had to admit he was itching for a confrontation. The past few days had been uneventful. He'd had nothing to take charge of, but nothing had been resolved, either.

They were approached by one of the partners. "Who's this?" the older man asked after greeting Marissa, working his bushy brows and mustache into a skeptical furor.

"Mr. Schnitzer, this is Jamie Wilson. He's an arts critic for the *Village Observer*. Jamie, Bill Schnitzer, senior partner." And serial overbiller, she'd once confided.

"Arts, hmm?" The man sounded as if he were confronting a plate of squid tentacles. "How does that pay?"

"In dollars," Jamie said, then coughed when Marissa stepped on his toe. "Exceedingly badly, sir."

"Heh," Schnitzer said, which was as much of a laugh as he seemed capable of. Marissa looked pleased.

They moved on. Jamie proceeded to discuss the movie version of *Rent* with Josephine Schnitzer, was licked up and down by Chelsea Howard's toy poodle and promised impossible-to-get theater tickets to her husband, who was in the doghouse after forgetting his wife's twenty-fifth birthday.

"Here," Marissa said, handing Jamie a glass of wine and a napkin wrapped around a slice of salmon and sprig of dill on pumpernickel. "You've earned it."

"I did good."

"Getting Frenched by a poodle is above and beyond." She risked a quick kiss. "You've become my most valuable asset."

"Behind every great woman is a guy who knows how to suck up."

"I take back what I said about you being a sexist. I think maybe you're my favorite man in the whole wide world."

His eyes flickered up and down her. "The feeling's mutual."

She moved closer, running her fingers over his hand in a teasing dance.

"How soon before we can get out of here?" he whispered.

"We haven't had dinner yet."

"Any chance of a quickie in a closet?"

"Only if you want to kill my chances of ever making partner."

Heaven forfend. "Then can we play footsie under the table?"

"I'll bet Chelsea is switching place cards as we speak. You made a conquest."

"She's married to her grandpa, what do you expect?"

"Shh. They're going in to dinner."

He squeezed her hand, holding her back from joining the others. "Now's our chance to slip out."

"You know I can't."

"No, of course not." She had no problem committing to her job. Only to him.

She winked. "But maybe we can leave a little early."

"And miss the senior partner's ethics lecture?" Jamie had spent a few minutes with the somewhat pompous Thomas Howard. While he admired the man for recognizing Marissa's value, Jamie couldn't see how she expected to conform to the firm's rigid expectations forever. She respected authority figures, but would never be a Stepford lawyer, obediently toeing the company line.

Legs like hers were made for kicking up a fuss.

ALLARD'S TIME HAD COME. Tonight, the White Star would be his.

Each day without her had been a torment. Never knowing with absolute certainty that she was safe, always standing guard. At times he'd questioned his objectivity. The money, after all, was supposed to be his motivation. Riches beyond his wildest dreams. The amulet was only a means to that end.

But it wasn't the money that called to him.

It was the White Star. She was in his blood—powerful, seductive, endlessly fascinating.

His employer had grown increasingly agitated with the wait. "Bring me the amulet," he'd ordered.

Allard had recoiled at the man's assumption of authority. He had agreed to the job, yes, but he worked alone. In darkness and shadow, beholden to no one.

La Souri Noire, came the whisper. His father's voice.

"I will finish it," Allard vowed. One million euros. A hundred times—a thousand times!—his father's best haul.

His confidence surged. Even the common thug who'd botched his own burglary hadn't prevented Allard's destiny—only delayed it.

Although he now had a copy of the keys to Marissa's apartment, and had her schedule down pat, he'd delayed until she was out for the evening to make his move. The wait was worth the familiarity he felt when using the cover of darkness, relying on no disguise but his skill at slipping in and out unseen.

He stood at Marissa's door, caressing it with his fingertips as he listened for sounds from within.

Silence. As planned, he could safely let himself in, assured that the blonde who'd unexpectedly answered his token knock on his first attempt to raid the apartment was long gone.

There was only the White Star. *So close now.*

The copy of the first key worked smoothly, but the

second stuck. He jiggled it, keeping a tight hold of his calm. There would be no more mistakes.

A creak sounded at the other end of the narrow hallway that ran along the stairwell leading upstairs. Allard's blood froze. Was it a floorboard? The opening of a door?

He didn't react, not wanting to appear startled. For all anyone knew, he was invited—a roommate, a brother, a lover, a friend. Acting surreptitiously would only make him stand out.

But he was no longer as composed. A firm twist got the key unstuck and he felt the bolt slide open. With the quickest of glances over his shoulder, he stepped inside and shut the door with a gentle *click.*

He'd been spotted! The nosy old crone next door had stuck her head into the hall.

Allard breathed deeply, trying to quiet his racing heart. No matter, he told himself. He was safe inside, silent and still in the darkness. He needed only seconds to retrieve the amulet and be on his way.

His eyes narrowed, tracing the layout of the apartment, meticulously planning his route even though it was blatantly apparent. He clung to the walls, gliding silently in the direction of the bedroom.

Almost there. He knelt at the foot of the bed and reached underneath for the suitcase.

Suddenly the damned cat attacked, slashing a paw at him from out of the dark, narrow space below the bed.

With a curse, Allard withdrew, propelling himself backward across the carpet. Where had the spiteful beast gone?

He looked for it, searching the corners, the top of the bed. Not a creature stirred. Except the mouse.

There was no time to hesitate. He put a hand over his head and crawled forward again. He'd grasped the handle of the bag and was pulling it toward himself when the cat let out a vicious yowl and leaped at him from above.

Needle-sharp claws bit into his face. He roared with pain and fury, flailing at the stiff, arched cat. It screeched and attacked again. Fur crackled with electricity. His skin tore. Desperately he gripped the lean, twisting body in his hands and flung the feline aside.

The cat landed with a thump and immediately scurried back under the bed.

Allard was stunned. His breathing was loud and harsh in the suddenly silent room.

The doorbell rang. A frantic pounding followed. "I've called the police," a female voice screeched. "They're on the way!"

Cringing, Allard fumbled once more for the suitcase.

The pocket was empty.

He swore, running his hands over every crevice. Nothing. The amulet had been removed.

The door rattled beneath the busybody's fist. *Bang, bang.*

Too much racket. He couldn't think. His vision was dimmed by blood and perspiration.

How could the amulet be gone? Every instinct said that Marissa hadn't found the treasure.

Perhaps it had fallen out. Warily, he reached beneath the bed, feeling through assorted items.

The cat hissed a warning and he jerked his hand away before it pounced. Now there were sirens in the distance.

Allard staggered to his feet. He wrenched at the iron bars over the window. No escape that way.

Though he was loathe to give up in spite of the cat, he saw no choice through the shock and pain and fear. He darted out of the room, one hand going for the knife in his pocket.

The sour, stinging tang of blood was on his tongue. It tasted like defeat.

MARISSA WAS LEAVING the powder room when she saw Paul disappear into a room farther along the hall. "What's this about?" he asked in a brooding tone, then shut the door before she heard the reply.

Typical, she thought, forgetting that she and Jamie had joked about ducking away themselves. Paul's date was a painfully skinny blonde who worked in advertising and had tried to run a focus group at the dinner table. Her voice pierced Marissa's eardrum like needle-nose pliers to the brain.

Low murmuring was coming from inside the room. Marissa crept closer. It would be even more typical if Paul had worked an assignation with another woman into his evening. What a creep.

She pressed her ear to the door.

"I have everything under control," Paul said from the other side, except that he didn't sound as confident as usual.

The responding voice was male, more distant, so she

couldn't tell who it was with any certainty. Perhaps Bradley Coffman? It was his house, after all.

Paul again. "No, I haven't been dodging. Just setting up the final details. There was no trouble in the Caymans. None at all."

Ah. Marissa backed away. Paul was being called on the carpet by one of the partners. While her unexpected departure might have thrown a monkey wrench in his schedule, she doubted that it would have caused him any significant trouble. Granted, he'd been worried what she'd seen of his late-night meeting. But what trouble could she cause? A client was a client, unless...

The client was a shady client.

How egocentric she'd been, thinking that Paul had been concerned with *her!* What he'd really cared about was being fingered for...for what?

She didn't believe the partners would knowingly engage in illegal doings. Paul might, especially if he was under the gun to keep his clients happy.

What *had* he been doing in the Caymans? Was that why he'd been so adamant about keeping her out of the way? Then coaxing her, almost threatening her...

The camera, she thought, remembering it lying broken on the floor, the film exposed.

The photos. She'd assumed they'd concerned Paul because she'd caught his indiscretion with the bimbo on film. But maybe not.

She wanted to return to eavesdropping to see if she could pick up a name, but Jamie called to her. "There you are." He came closer. "Do you think it's too early to go? They've finished with dessert."

"Yes, let's go." She hurriedly pulled him away before Paul heard them. "I've had an epiphany," she whispered, "but we can't talk about it here."

"An epiphany about us?" he asked hopefully.

She wanted to say yes, if only to see the joy in his face. But she couldn't.

"About the burglary." She looked for the Coffmans, finding only their hostess, and thanked her for the lovely evening.

Minutes later, she and Jamie were in a cab heading south. "It's the photos!" she said excitedly. "That's what the burglar wanted."

Jamie frowned. "The film was ruined."

"Yes, but that was a new film, remember? I'd already removed the one from my vacation."

"Then if it was in your apartment, how do you know the thief didn't take it?"

"Because the film wasn't there. I'd dropped it off to be developed after I got home. In all the uproar since then, I forgot. It's still at the camera store, waiting to be picked up."

"Okay, that makes sense. But what's on this film that's so valuable a burglar would want it?"

"The pictures will be worth plenty if they prove to be incriminating."

"Explain."

She angled toward him, knocking their knees. "Do you remember when I said I saw Paul on the beach?"

She waited for Jamie's nod. "He was meeting with a client, which seemed unusual. But, stupid me—" she rapped her knuckles against her skull "—I let myself get distracted by the bimbo's presence."

"Aha," Jamie said. "She's the red herring."

"Exactly. The important thing was that I happened to snap a few shots of her and Paul. I won't know for sure until I get the photos, but it's possible the client was also in the frame. Whether or not he actually is, I think *Paul* is afraid he might be."

Jamie took her hand, saying everything he needed to with one firm squeeze. "What happened tonight to give you this epiphany?"

"I overheard Paul talking with one of the partners. Coffman, I believe. I didn't see him in the living room when I returned. They were discussing the trip to the Caymans and it seemed as if Paul was under some duress to wrap things up there."

"What kind of things?"

"That, I don't know. A good guess would be that it has to do with clients who have incorporated their company there. Or perhaps it concerned a transfer of funds, for tax benefits." When she got the chance, she'd look into the list of Paul's clients. Nose around, see what the office gossip said.

Jamie was looking out at the traffic, his mouth grim. "You think the partners are involved?"

"I suppose that's possible, but there was no indication from what I overheard. Whoever it was only seemed to ask him to get the work done. Paul was defending himself, saying that there'd been no trouble. If he's done something illicit, it's probably his own idea. Or the client's." She tried to be fair. "But that's a big *if.* We don't know anything for sure."

"Except that Paul Beckwith is amoral." By now, Jamie's entire expression had gone stony.

"Well, yes." Even though Marissa hadn't known the extent of Paul's treachery in the beginning, she was ashamed that she'd ever been involved with the man.

Jamie had followed her train of thought. "I *am* a dork. I should have told you about him and Shandi right at the start."

"Let's not beat ourselves up with recriminations." She leaned into him. "Full speed ahead, isn't that the motto?"

"With caution."

"Yes, with caution."

They had pulled up in front of their building. Jamie climbed out, then held the door for Marissa. He paid the driver, signaling for him to wait a moment. "I don't suppose we can pick up the photos now?"

"The camera shop is closed. It's not a twenty-four-hour place." She waved the cab on.

They met another tenant as they let themselves into the building. Mrs. Pankowski from 3B, standing in the hall with a baseball bat in one hand and a taser in the other. She switched off the taser and dropped it into the roomy pocket of her housecoat. "You two missed all the excitement."

"What happened?" Jamie said.

"I spotted a stranger letting himself into your apart-ment. He looked surprised to see me so I called the fuzz. He knocked me down, busting out through the door. I don't hold with all these goings-on. This is supposed to be a good neighborhood! A good building!" She glared accusingly at them.

"I'm so sorry," Marissa said. "Are you hurt?"

"Nah. But *he* was. Blood all over his face." Mrs. Pankowski cracked a lipless grin. "The cops were crawling all over the building and the streets, but they didn't catch the bastard."

Marissa grabbed Jamie's sleeve. "Harry had better be okay. We should have left Sally to guard him."

"Or vice versa." Jamie asked Mrs. Pankowski about the police findings, but she had nothing else to share except an admonition that they should cause no more noise and fuss. Marissa and Jamie hurried upstairs.

She handed the keys to Jamie and pulled out her cell phone, which she'd kept switched off during the dinner party. One of her messages was from Officer O'Connor. "There was a confirmed break-in," she relayed to Jamie. "The super met the responding officers at my apartment to check out the place. It's okay for us to go in."

"Did he say anything about the suspect?"

She snapped the phone shut. "Just that they narrowly missed him, but they got a description from Mrs. Pankowski."

Jamie turned the key. "He must have been watching the place and knew you'd gone out for the evening."

"There's a cheery thought."

They entered. Jamie flipped on the light. Marissa crowded in behind him, holding on to him with a finger crooked through one of the belt loops of his best dress trousers. "Harry? Kitty, kitty?"

A muffled meow came from the back of the apartment. Marissa hurried into the bedroom. She peered under the bed. "Harry!"

The cat crawled out, wearing a dust ball between his flattened ears. His whiskers twitched. "Poor little guy." She brushed him off, then fluffed up his long white fur. "When this is over, you'll never want to be left home again, will you, kitty?"

"Marissa," Jamie said from behind her.

She stopped crooning to the cat and looked up. "What?"

"You do realize, that if your theory is correct, you're saying that Paul sent the burglars to your home."

She narrowed her eyes. "Yes, I do realize that."

"To go that far…for a pack of photos?" He shook his head. "Paul would have had to be involved in something very serious, and very illegal. When you go back to work, don't get into it with him, in any way, shape or form."

"I'll be cautious."

"No. You'll do nothing. We'll pick up the photos in the morning and if there's anything there, we'll turn them over to the police."

"What about my career?"

"Screw your career. I want you alive."

"No one's going to kill me!"

"Damn right, because it won't come to that. I promise I won't let it come to that."

Marissa shivered, holding Harry so tightly he mewled in protest.

12

"MARISSA SUAREZ," Jamie said to the counter person at the tiny camera shop. "S-U-A—"

"Got it." The girl slid the envelope of photos across the counter and took the money Marissa offered. They hurried out without waiting for change.

"Put them in your purse," Jamie directed, feeling slightly foolish as he checked up and down the street. They'd put on "disguises"—sunglasses and a bandanna tied pirate-style for him, jeans, sneakers and a shapeless sweater for Marissa. Her hair was knotted in a bun, hidden under a wide-brimmed sun hat.

"I want to see." She shoved the packet into her straw bag. "The suspense is killing me."

"Wait until we get to Havana."

Hand-in-hand, they sped to her favorite hangout spot and managed to snag one of the booths with high carved wood seats that gave them a sense of enclosed privacy. Marissa peeped around the side. "Were we followed?"

Jamie was watching the door. "Sit back." No one came in after them except a lean greyhound of a woman dressed in clinging workout clothes. She collapsed onto one of the wrought-iron bar stools.

"That's Bebe," Marissa said. "She runs marathons."

"Can't you stay out of sight?"

"Sor-ry!" she sang, settling back. "Can I look now? Forget that. I'm looking."

"Here's the waitress." He quickly ordered citron pressé. It was too early for lunch even though they'd left his apartment at nine-thirty and taken a roundabout journey to the camera shop, including stops at a Laundromat, a pharmacy and a clothing store. All to throw off invisible lurkers.

Marissa ripped into the packet. She tossed a handful of the photos aside, spraying them across the tabletop. Vistas of the blue-green ocean and white sand beach, brown bodies in the sun.

He separated out a shot of Marissa sitting under a thatched roof in a skimpy bikini top and sarong, then put it back. Paul had probably snapped it.

She flipped through a series of sunset photos. Pink and orange ribbons in a dark sky. Her lashes had flicked when he lingered over her photo. "That shot was taken right before he ditched me at the tiki bar for the last time."

She returned to the other photos. "Here we go." They hunched over the table. "Take a look at these."

Marissa passed him a copy of the first snapshot. The lighting wasn't good. Paul's back was to the camera, a woman plastered to his side. She was made of curves and pink lips and a head of hair so yellow it was almost fluorescent. A third figure was indistinct.

"This one's better," she said.

Paul and the other man were speaking in the second photo. The client had stepped forward into the light source, but his head was down, exhibiting a bald spot the size of a dinner plate. He wore a casual white shirt, unbuttoned almost to the waist, khakis and sandals, with a large gold watch on his right wrist. Just a man on vacation, except for the Halliburton case clutched at his side.

"Not good enough. You can't see his face."

Marissa frowned as she looked at the remaining two photos. One she discarded as being too murky to be helpful. The other she held close to her nose, squinting. "Bingo."

"Let's see." They studied the photo between them. Paul and the woman were prominent, but in the background the other man looked on, smiling in a rather sleazy, voyeuristic way. "Recognize him?" Jamie asked.

"Nope. I've never seen him in the office, but then the firm has so many clients I've met only a small percentage of them."

He considered. "Even if we do identify the man, these photos aren't proof of anything."

"I guess not." Marissa sighed. "I was so sure that we'd find something incriminating."

"Me, too," he admitted. "I was having *Alias* fantasies."

She looked up with a grin. "Well, you do look good in your disguise."

"I look like an idiot." He returned to the photos, picking up the one she'd rejected. "I just can't figure out why Paul would be desperate to take these from you."

"That depends on who the guy is. Maybe an underworld hit man or a deposed island dictator." She waved a hand at his look of skepticism. "I could come up with lots of scenarios. But the point to remember is that even if Paul doesn't know for sure what the photos show, he *believed* they might be harmful."

"No one else will care."

"The partners might. Especially Thomas Howard. He's practically my mentor. He'll listen."

Jamie glanced up. "Assuming the firm's not involved."

Marissa clutched her elbows, which she'd rested on the table. "You're trying to scare me."

Tenderness softened his tone. "I'm trying to keep you safe." He went back to the photo in his hand. "What do we do now?"

She gathered the others into a pile and returned them to the envelope. "I doubt the police would be interested. Let's think on it over the rest of the weekend."

"Want to skip the play this afternoon?"

"Um. No, let's go. Sitting around my apartment waiting for the next burglary attempt won't do us any good." To be safe, she'd moved Harry and his accoutrements to Jamie's place for the duration.

"I'm sorry that—" Jamie stopped and blinked. The photo he'd been studying was a dud. Dark and grainy. The two men were only blurred shapes, but he was able to make out the client because of his white shirt. Then there was the silver briefcase the mystery man had carried in the first photos of the sequence.

Now in Paul's possession.

"These photos are in order?" Jamie asked, lining them up.

Marissa checked the negatives. "Yes."

"Then why does Paul have the briefcase? Did you ever see him with it before that night?"

She shook her head. "Do you think it was an exchange?"

"I don't know what to think. But I'd sure like to know what's in that briefcase."

MARISSA SURPRISED JAMIE when she caught his arm outside the Chelsea theater, which was actually an old shoe store converted into a multiuse space. Beneath a giant faded ad for Florsheim shoes was a marquee that read Backslash Video Productions/ChelBro Art School/Funkytown Players Theater.

He thought she was about to suggest ducking out on the play before they got inside. Instead she put her chin on his shoulder and said, "Let's forget everything else and pretend we're on a date. Are you game?"

Was he game? Hell, yeah. In fact, he couldn't have asked for a better sign from her.

He cleared his clogged throat. "I'd like that." But suddenly he was nervous. After all this time, how did he act on a date with Marissa?

He saw a florist across the street. "Wait here for two seconds," he said, leaving her outside the theater with her pretty dress and blinking lashes.

Five minutes later he gave her a small bundle of flowers. Freesia and lilies, the woman had suggested when he'd asked for a sweet-smelling bouquet. "You're the kind of date I'd bring flowers to."

"What a romantic you are," she said. She might have been blushing a little. "I'm glad I rank so well."

"Top of the list, babe."

"They smell so good. Thank you."

He offered his arm. "Shall we go inside?"

"Certainly, kind gentleman."

They joined the small trickle of ticket holders entering the theater and found their seats in a narrow shoebox of a room. Marissa looked around her, past the shabbiness to the faux-painted murals of cartoon theatergoers. She kept sniffing the flowers. And smiling at him.

He didn't know what to say. He was dating Marissa and he'd reverted to his tongue-tied high school days. "Uh." He swallowed. "So tell me. If I'd asked you on a date when we first met, what would you have said?"

She hesitated with her head cocked. He knew she'd tell the truth. Why the hell had he asked the question?

"I would have said yes."

"I don't think so. You only dated a certain type of man then."

"Yes, and you know why? That's who approached me. Successful businessmen. The interesting, arty types never asked. *You* didn't."

"True."

"I'll concede that I became accustomed to certain expectations in a date. But I was never one of those women who'd turn her nose up at picnics in the park or Italian ices at a softball game." She nudged him with her elbow. "Actually, if you think about it, that was the kind of stuff I always did with you."

He raised his brows. "So we've been dating all along?"

She smiled. "It seems so. But you never brought me flowers before." She took another sniff of the bouquet. He could smell the sweetness, too, and it was making him heady. Especially when she leaned in as the lights dimmed and said in his ear, "I'm glad you finally stepped up your game."

After that, he relaxed and enjoyed the date.

The play, an overenthusiastic revival of *Guys and Dolls,* would have been a bust if he hadn't been with Marissa, who shared his sense of the absurd. When the

actor who played Nathan Detroit came on stage in a
shiny purple zoot suit, they couldn't look at each other.
Miss Adelaide's gyrations at the Hot Box put them over
the top. Marissa had pinched his arm until he stopped
snorting and choking back laughter.

Afterward they went to dinner at a familiar neighborhood trattoria with candlelit and linen-draped tables.
Between courses, she "helped" him with his notes for
the review. By the time dessert arrived, they were
played out and sitting in pleasant, companionable
silence.

"I'm glad we haven't lost this," he said, carving off
a bit of his tiramisu to offer her.

"Calorie gorging? That's why I work out so often."
Her lips closed around the sweet bite. "Mmm, yummy."

Watching her mouth pucker and release was almost
obscene. His blood thickened. Even with all the drama and
danger they'd undergone since getting together, she could
have him stimulated beyond belief in under five seconds.

"You know what I mean. We're still friends."

"Friends with benefits," she said in a lilting tone it
was hard to take exception with.

But he did. "Friends and lovers." He nudged her foot
under the table. "Remember, we're dating now. Don't
act like I'm just your bed buddy."

She smiled over the rim of her wineglass. "No, that
would be our pets."

All right. She'd accepted the date, even though she
was still determined to avoid his attempts at a serious
moment. *Some* progress had been made.

Time would be his ally. When she finally recognized
that he wasn't going anywhere, unlike her past lovers,

he'd be ensconced so deeply in her life that she wouldn't be able to separate him from her from them.

"I know what you mean," she said. "We always have a good time together. It's just that now that happens to include unclothed fun, too." She brushed her foot against his ankle. "Honestly, you're the best boyfriend I've ever had. I like the boy, I like the friend, I like everything about you."

Not a declaration of undying love, but it would do.

"Guess what?" he said, feeling very pleased that more progress had been made than he'd first thought. "I get better as time goes by."

"Better?" She fanned her face. "I don't know if I can stand the excitement."

"You're holding up well so far."

"And you—" Her foot, sans shoe, slipped beneath his pant leg. Her warm little toes pattered against his calf. She was a dexterous girl. "You surprise me. Always rising to the occasion."

He made a gruff sound in his throat. "Eat your dessert."

Her foot retreated. She took a bite of her ricotta cheesecake, watching his face as she licked the fork with a catlike tongue. Her hair hung in loose waves across her shoulders, the ends brushing over the curves of her breasts every time she moved. Her dress was the color of pale morning sunlight, cut straight across the top with narrow straps around her shoulders. In contrast, her skin was almost golden, warmed by the dancing flame of the candle. A small pair of diamonds winked at her ears. The dainty gold crucifix dangled near her cleavage. Looking at her made him fill up with love.

"You know, there could be anything in that briefcase,"

she said out of the blue. He thought she was purposely deflecting the mood until her foot touched his thigh.

He caught her heel before she went any further.

Her face remained guileless. "Papers, files. It doesn't have to be money or drugs or whatever you're thinking."

"You're still defending Paul."

"Maybe I don't want him to be irredeemably bad."

He jiggled her foot. "No reflection on you."

"Pah. You know when to lie. I like that about you." Her foot squirmed out of his grasp. "See what I mean? I have bad judgment." The nimble toes rubbed his thigh. "I'm rash, I'm wild, I'm headstrong."

The sole of her foot pressed firmly against the fullness at his fly. She blinked. "Are you headstrong? I think you are. You just hide it well."

"Marissa." He closed his legs, squeezing her foot between them. "Let's get out of here."

"I seem to have lost my shoe. Want to dive under and find it?"

"I'd find more than your shoe."

"Promises, promises. It's a ballet flat with a practical low heel. I never wear high heels when there's a chance I might have to run for my life."

He released her foot. "Don't even joke about that."

She was smiling. Glowing. "It's going to be all right, Jamie. Somehow, I'm sure of that. Ever since the airport, when I saw you in a brand-new way, I've had this knowledge. A confidence that we're…oh, I don't know, maybe destined to be."

Leaps and bounds of progress.

"To be what?" he asked, swinging for the fences.

Her mouth curved into a smile. "That's all. To *be*. No question."

To be together, he thought. She still wouldn't say it, but he could wait. She'd already given him more than he'd expected.

THERE WAS A FEELING between them tonight that was different. A little scary, but very arousing. Tantalizing in its purest form, as headily intoxicating as champagne bubbles rising in a flute.

Marissa felt as if she could fly.

Jamie took her hand, pulling her close to him with a strength she hadn't expected. She let out a little "Oh!" of resistance, but then let herself melt. Aside from the little stumble when she declared this a date, he was so sure and confident these days. All that overprotective, macho testosterone.

"Don't look now," he said, "but someone may be following us."

She stiffened her neck, trying not to turn when every instinct demanded it. "Who?"

"I don't know. I only caught a glimpse of a man's reflection in a window. I might be paranoid."

"I want to look."

"No use. If he's really following us, he's staying far back."

"Come with me," she said. They hurried along West 4th to Washington Square Park, where leafy trees overhung rows of iron benches and fence. Still fighting her instincts, but this time to keep running, Marissa sat, pulling Jamie down beside her. Her heart was pounding double-time as she turned toward him. She reached for his face.

"What are you doing?" he blurted right before she kissed him.

"Shush. Keep kissing me."

His hands tightened on her back as he pulled her in. She closed her eyes, not even fighting it, and let the kiss take over. For a minute. A surprisingly glorious minute, considering that she wasn't supposed to be thinking about the kiss at all.

After another minute—she was weak—she cracked an eye, trying to see past Jamie's head. There were a number of people out enjoying the perfect evening. One passerby smiled at her; another looked away. Most barely noticed, but a group of boys with skateboards watched avidly as they scooted back and forth, twirling and flipping their boards.

No sign of anyone shadowing them.

She closed her eyes again. "Keep kissing me."

"No problem," he muttered. "But our guy's no fool."

She was. A fool for love, or some facsimile of it. Why else would she be getting so turned on? Had to be the crazy hormones, shooting her brain full of a volatile, giddy infatuation.

"Kiss my neck," she crooned. His warm lips and tongue worked their way lower, titillating her nerve endings so that she felt her skin light up like a glittering fireworks show. It was becoming difficult to keep her mind on the plan.

Her head fell back, her neck arched. Only because in that position, she was able to watch the street through her lashes.

They'd lingered a long while over dinner, but the light had held on as the days grew longer. An amber dusk was falling across the park, hushed and beautiful, for the moment held at bay by the lights along the street.

At last she saw the sign she'd been waiting for. The brief flame of a match or a lighter, instantly lost when the figure turned away. The spy was sticking to the shadows cast by the trees.

She waited. Jamie's tongue licked along her collarbone. His thumb stroked beneath her breast.

Her nostrils flared, trying to catch the scent of tobacco. Something about the odor was unique, perhaps even familiar.

He was too far away. She dropped her head forward to whisper into Jamie's ear. "I think I saw him. I can't be sure he's following us."

"What for? What do we know?"

"It's what we have—the photos." They were in the breast pocket of Jamie's jacket. The negatives were in a Ziploc bag at the bottom of Sally's dog food.

He pondered that with a pleated forehead. "Doesn't feel right. The parts don't add up."

"Ah, that's the intriguing puzzle of it." She kissed his cheek, trying to get another glimpse of their follower. No luck. "You know, we're sitting ducks, like we were that night on the street when he went for my suitcase. Should we hop in a cab?"

"Exactly my point. Paul didn't know about the photos when that happened."

She was too intoxicated to concentrate on details as they walked out of the park. "There's a cab." She raised a hand to hail it.

Jamie caught her wrist. "No, let's run. That will tell us if he's really following us or if I'm seeing things."

"I'm game."

They went flying down the street, crossing under the cherry tree at the Thompson Street entrance. Pigeons flapped across the sidewalk. Pedestrians dodged out of the way.

They slowed at the corner, turning it instead of waiting to cross with the light, then picking up the pace again. There was a break in traffic and Jamie stepped off the curb, pulling her along.

At the other side, Jamie's head swiveled back the way they'd come. "Is he following us?" she asked between gasps.

"Yes. Come on."

They put on another burst of speed.

They turned another corner, gradually pulling up as they reached the midblock point. Jamie turned, searching the pedestrians, even the cabs that slowed and honked. "I don't see him."

Marissa looked up at a large stone Presbyterian church looming nearby. "Let's go in here." She tugged on Jamie's hand. "Quick. Before he sees us."

They raced up the circular cement steps and pushed through the heavy double doors into the narthex. Bountiful bouquets of creamy roses and tulips decorated the space. Two tall floor candelabras flanked the doors into the church proper, which reverberated with the stirring strains of organ music.

"A church service," Jamie said.

"A wedding," Marissa guessed. Her heels tapped across the stone floor. "Let's take a peek."

"We shouldn't interrupt."

"We'll be quiet as mice." She put her finger up to her lips, then eased open the door. A glowing light spilled out. The music expanded, accompanied by voices raised in song.

"It's beautiful," she whispered to Jamie, who was looking over her shoulder. A white carpet ran up an aisle trimmed with more of the flowers and candles. The pews were almost filled, only those at the back of the church left open. She nodded to the front of the church. "Look."

Beneath the high arched beams and gilded decor of the altar, a bride and groom stood in a pool of candlelight, holding hands as the hymn ended. The guests sat to the sound of rustling silk. A minister garbed in black and white began speaking about the sanctity of marriage.

An usher appeared at the door. "Bride or groom?"

Jamie stepped back, but she grabbed hold of his sleeve. "Bride," she said, tiptoeing inside and slipping into the very last pew.

Jamie joined her. "What if—"

"Shh." Whether it was the sanctified aura of the church, or the intimacy of the marriage ceremony, she was cocooned in a sense of warm, safe serenity. Her body settled, her mind calmed. When she looked at Jamie, she saw that he felt it too. His eyes were large, dark, flecked with the reflections of the candlelight. He reached for her hand.

Somehow, it seemed inevitable that they'd ended up here.

And very right.

The bride and groom radiated with their love for

each other as they took their vows. Marissa didn't hear every word, but she felt them inside herself, resonating with a strength and reverence that was greater—far greater—than her previous reluctance to accept an emotional need she couldn't control. One that might overwhelm her. That would surely change everything about the way she looked at the world.

She and Jamie looked at each other at the same moment. She studied his face as if this were the first time she'd ever seen it. He was bravery, goodness, sex and compassion. And so much more.

I'm in love with him.

Their linked hands gripped tighter. She felt her heart expanding to accept Jamie's love for her, and hers for him. It was a pure love, a true love.

Deeper than the earth's very core.

Longer than time itself.

When the minister pronounced the couple at the altar husband and wife, it was Marissa and Jamie who kissed first.

ON THE STEPS outside the church, despair overtook the seething anger that Jean Allard had contained for so long. He hurried away without caring where he went.

They had toyed with him. Like a cat played with a mouse, teasing and taunting, giving him a moment's hope only to snatch it away.

He'd known in his heart that they didn't carry the amulet, but he no longer trusted himself. He'd followed them on a fool's errand all around the city on the remote chance that they had found the treasure and intended to bring it to the authorities.

Too long, he thought bitterly. The White Star had been out of his grasp for too long. It was slipping away.

The bloodred scratches across his face were a constant, pulsing reminder that he had failed, and failed again. There seemed no more opportunity for him to get into the girl's apartment. She was on guard now. She was defended.

Allard sped up his pace. His mind darted, wriggled, burrowed, searching for one small opening. One speck of light.

Suddenly he saw it. An answer so simple it was genius.

He *wanted* Marissa Suarez to find the amulet.

When she did, when she stepped onto the street with the White Star in her possession, she would be vulnerable. Even if the boyfriend was there.

Allard reached into his pants' pocket. He turned the knife over in his palm, cradling its lethal promise.

The White Star was his.

He'd killed for much less.

13

MARISSA HOVERED in the doorway to the senior partner's office, watching Thomas Howard as he wielded a pen over a contract, striking out sections with heavy slashes as he dictated notes at the same time. Her stomach roiled. She'd timed her visit when Mr. Howard's executive assistant was on break. This conversation must be as private as possible.

She cleared her throat to gain his attention. "Mr. Howard? May I speak to you?"

He looked up. "Marissa! Certainly." He stood, gesturing her toward a chair. "Please sit."

"Thank you." She smoothed her skirt across the back of her thighs and sat in one of the webbed white-leather-and-aluminum chairs that faced his desk. The box-shaped chair bristled with steel braces and bolts, looking strangely like a cross between a straitjacket and an electric chair. The comparison was not a comforting thought.

"How can I help you, Marissa?" Mr. Howard asked. He was gray-haired, bespectacled and smiling. Even though she considered him to be a friend, in a stern, fatherly way, she suddenly felt as flustered—and determined—as when she'd asked her mother's kindly gynecologist for birth control.

"I have a problem, Mr. Howard."

"I'll be happy to help." He folded his hands atop the desk. "But you must remember to call me Thomas."

"Yes, sir. Thomas." She swallowed. "It's about Paul Beckwith."

Behind chrome glasses with blue lenses, Howard's eyes took on a speculative gleam. "Personal problems?"

She flushed. "Not exactly. It is a delicate situation." Jamie had told her to wait, but she wanted the photos out of her hands. The entire affair, really.

She began. "Perhaps you know that I accompanied Paul to the Cayman Islands recently."

Howard made a noncommittal sound. Probably thinking of keeping neutral in the likelihood of a sexual harassment suit.

"He was conducting business meetings there."

Howard smiled as if she were a ten-year-old visiting his office on Take Your Children to Work day. "We have clients with Cayman connections. The firm often does business in the Caribbean. Nothing untoward in that."

"No, of course not. I wouldn't have thought anything of it, if not for—" She tried to think how to put her suspicions. Better to simply state the facts.

She laid the envelope of photos on his desk. "I took these from the hotel balcony."

Howard thumbed through them. "I see."

"I have no idea who the client is, and I don't really want to know."

"I'm not following your intention, Marissa. Are you suggesting that Paul's business with this man was not aboveboard?" He pushed the photos around on his desk blotter. "I see nothing particularly troublesome. Is it the woman? She is rather, uh, obvious, shall we say? I'm sure you have reason to be displeased."

Ugh! "No, that's not it, sir." Marissa gripped the arms of the torture chair.

The senior partner cocked his head. "Then you'll have to tell me."

"If you'll examine the photos closely, you can see that Paul appears to receive the other man's briefcase."

Howard glanced down, then cocked his thumbs into the air before refolding them behind his knitted fingers. *So?*

Marissa's father had used the same gesture when she was a little girl. In a very different context. *This is the church, here is the steeple. Open the doors and see all the people.*

"I thought that seemed suspicious," she said.

"I'm sure there's a good explanation."

"Yes, I'd agree, if not for—" Again, she hesitated. If this went badly, she was putting her job in jeopardy. Certainly her advancement.

What, are you afraid? Go ahead. Plunge.

"Mr. How—Thomas. There have been incidents."

He looked troubled. "What do you mean?"

"A mugging attempt on the street. Two break-ins at my apartment. I've been followed."

"And you believe these events are…?"

"Connected to the photos, yes."

"Why is that?"

"Because—" She frowned. "I'm not quite sure. But Paul seemed concerned that I'd taken the pictures and that was when the trouble started. Too much of a coincidence, I think."

Howard huffed. "Did Paul threaten you?"

"Not really. He asked me not to bring this into the office."

"Yet you are."

"Yes, but I'm not making an accusation. There's no proof, other than the photos, and they're open to interpretation. I only wanted to give them to you, sir, and let you handle the matter."

"I see." Howard gathered the photographs. "I'll speak to Paul about this client. He won't be bothering you again, Marissa, you can be certain of that. I apologize on behalf of the firm for any upset you've suffered."

Marissa's spine stiffened. She was getting the brush-off. "I'm fine, sir."

The lawyer smiled, less kindly than before. His eyes now seemed as steely as the frames of his spectacles. "You've always been an excellent employee. Let's not allow a minor hiccup in judgment to affect your position here at Howard, Coffman."

"No reason it should," she said, rising.

He nodded.

There was a moment of heavy silence.

"I'll expect to hear from you then, regarding your—" *Investigation* was too strong a word. She managed a neutral smile as she stood. "Regarding your inquiry of Paul."

Again, the glint of steel. "That you will."

"Thank you." She turned to walk out.

Howard stopped her. "Just a moment, Marissa. Do you have the negatives?"

"Why do you need the negatives?"

"Need? I wouldn't use that word. I have no particular requirement of them, but it seems prudent in the name of thoroughness."

"Yes, I suppose." She contemplated his request for a lengthy pause, wondering if she could make him squirm. Nope. Not the smallest tic. Maybe she was being needlessly suspicious. "The negatives should be in the envelope."

He peered beneath the flap. "Ah, so they are."

"I also believe in being thorough." Marissa nodded. "Good day, Thomas."

She walked out, smiling to herself. Luckily, she was so thorough that she always got double prints.

"CAN'T SLEEP AGAIN?" Jamie asked.

"I thought it was that lumpy sofa bed keeping me up." After the first sleepless night, Marissa had insisted they spend a night at her apartment, in relative comfort. "Maybe I have insomnia."

"Maybe."

She sighed.

He waited.

"It's been two days. And nothing!"

"What did you expect?"

"That Paul would storm into my office, if nothing else. Raging at me for getting him into trouble."

"Does that mean he's *not* in trouble?"

"Perhaps. Then again, Mr. Howard may not have questioned him because he didn't take me seriously. Who knows?" She twisted onto her side, muttering, "Certainly not me."

"How come you haven't come right out and asked Howard what the hell is up?"

She put the back of her hand over her eyes. "Trying to be patient."

"I'd rather you could sleep."

"Me, too. It's not easy being passive."

He chuckled. "Some people call it cooperation."

"Cooperation sucks."

"Look at it this way. There haven't been any more incidents."

"Oh, I'm thrilled." Her face turned toward the window. "Does that mean I can get the burglar bars removed?"

"Not yet." Not ever, if he had a say.

"Harry doesn't like them either. He stalks them."

"Harry's been very edgy lately."

"Kind of like you."

"Me? Edgy?"

"Uh-huh."

"At least I haven't peed in the closet."

She laughed. "No, but how many times did you check the locks before bed?"

"I'm taking care of you."

She rolled up against him. "We're partners. We can take care of each other."

His hand went to her hip, which was bare except for the elastic of her string bikini panties. "Mmm, sounds good to me."

She kissed his chest. "Isn't sex supposed to be a sleeping pill?"

"Hasn't worked on you yet," he said, "but I'm willing to keep trying."

They snuggled against each other, their legs and arms entwining in a way that had become second nature in a very short time. Unless he added up the previous three years.

Since the evening of the church wedding, Marissa had been more comfortable with expressions of affection. They both knew that they'd taken a major step that night, but so far neither of them had attempted to put it into words.

He was more patient than Marissa.

She stroked his upper arm, her fingers tracing patterns around the muscles. "If Howard doesn't come through, I'll have to try something else."

"We can always go to the police, the way I wanted to. Give them a chance to look into it."

"My career would be over."

"Not your entire career. But, yeah, maybe this one job." He planted kisses along her forehead. "You have to decide what you're willing to put up with, or do, to stay there."

"There are compromises in every job. I've already

had to represent clients whose business ethics weren't my personal taste."

"Did you say *compromise?* Not unlike cooperation."

She went silent. He felt her breathing against his neck. Sensed the fight inside her.

Her hand dropped to the waistband of his boxers. "I get what you're saying. And I am willing to risk a lot. But going to the police would truly be career suicide. When I close my eyes, I see myself back in Miami, working out of a shabby storefront, making out wills for old men in Madras shorts and black socks."

"Come on. That won't happen." He grazed her with his lips. "And what if it did? Would that be so bad?"

"Hell, yes!"

"If I was there?"

"That would make it better. Tolerable."

"Only tolerable?"

"I don't think there's anything wrong with a woman wanting both a career and a hus—a fam—a satisfying love life."

"Yeah, I hear those hus-fams are very satisfying."

She giggled, playing with the tag on his shorts, running her finger along the puckered elastic. "So I'm exaggerating. There's a point in there somewhere."

"Yes," he conceded. "But for the short term, let's focus on the next few days. There's not much you can do if your boss doesn't want to bother with the photos."

Her hand slipped inside his boxer shorts. "I could get more evidence."

"How?"

"I'll nose around. Ophelia knows everything that goes down." She licked at his nipple as her hand closed on his growing erection.

He groaned.

"What was that groan for?" Her tongue swirled in his navel. "This?" Hot blood surged toward his loins. "Or my plan?"

He put his hand on the back of her head. "It's a plan now, is it?"

"I'll be careful." She pumped his erection, knowing he needed the firm pressure. His hips lifted, thrust. Her lips opened, sucking the head of his penis into the satin warmth of her mouth. Her tongue rolled, circled, plunged. He slid deeper into heaven. What was left of his brain reeled like a carnival ride.

Unbelievable. A blow job in the middle of the night. He had to marry this woman or die trying.

Her head lifted. "Give it to me," she said in a hoarse voice, her fist squeezing his shaft.

He thrust. She took him. Again and again, the driving instinct escalating until he was lost in a wet, dark world where there was only her hands and her sweet mouth and the love that he wanted to give to her, the love that she would learn to return, the love that was too big for words, for sex, for the humble human heart.

But that was all they had.

Marissa beckoned, taking him to the edge with her relentless, licentious mouth. He closed his eyes and saw lush greenery, a blazing sun, the golden-brown curves of a woman's naked body. Love. Truth. Destiny. Paradise.

With an animal cry, he dove into the raging torrent of his release, tumbling over the edge like a waterfall. His pulsing cock touched the back of her throat and she swallowed convulsively, the liquid movement of her mouth and tongue the only remaining touchstone in a capsized universe.

The rush!

He floated. Brainless. Undone.

Eventually he became aware of Marissa, her hot skin. The tantalizing peak, the roundness of her breast. Swaying beneath his hand.

She was kissing a path up his sprawled body.

"Sleepy yet?" he said, and her laugh was husky with sex.

"That would be you."

"What are you trying to do? Put me out for the count so I can make no objections to your great plan to play the innocent heroine who stumbles onto evidence and gets captured and held over a vat of snapping crocodiles while the hero is shot at when he comes to save her?"

She dug her chin into his abdomen until he winced. "I must not give head as good as I thought if you can put together a sentence like that afterward."

"Did it make sense?"

"Not particularly, unless there really are crocodiles in the sewers of New York. Therefore, I'm ignoring you."

His hands sank into her hair as he kissed her. Their legs tangled.

Keep her close.

"Am I going to have to chain you to this bed?"

"Ooh. Sounds like fun."

"Or I could pin you like a butterfly."

"Oh? Impalement?"

His chest expanded. "That's right."

She stretched out flat. "Might work."

He rolled over onto her, running his hands down her body. Instead of the sleep shirt, she wore a tiny tank. Her skin was incredibly smooth. He would never get enough of touching her.

"You'd need a day off from work," she mused. "And extraordinary staying power."

"I'll give it a try."

She made a sound of approval as he palmed her breast, molding it for his mouth. He sucked her nipple against his tongue.

She twisted her shoulders. Lifted one of her racy thoroughbred legs and wrapped it around his waist.

He thought of her running through the streets of New York, skirt flying, hair flowing. She'd been on an adrenaline high when they were followed into the church, but the next time she might not be so lucky.

And there would be a next time, knowing Marissa, even if turning in the photos had halted further attempts from the bad guys' end. She wouldn't let the puzzle rest there, unsolved.

With a wet smack, he plucked his lips from her breast. "If you could identify the client," he offered, "I'll research him. That might get us somewhere."

"Now you're thinking."

He sighed. "Promise me you won't put yourself into a dangerous spot."

"I'll send Ophelia instead," she joked.

"Seriously, Marissa. Be discreet."

"Yes, sir."

"Why don't I believe you?"

"Because I'm never compliant?"

"That'd do it. Not cooperative or compromising either."
She burrowed into him. "You know you like it."

Too much to let her go, he decided, enfolding her
in his arms.

He'd been waiting for this showdown, and finally the
time had come.

THAT AFTERNOON, Marissa called Ophelia into her
office. "What did you find out?"

They had scanned, enlarged and cropped the best of
the Cayman Islands photos, eliminating Paul and the
blonde for the sake of discretion. Ophelia had then
e-mailed the resulting closeup of the mystery client to
half a dozen carefully selected assistants in various de-
partments of the firm, asking for an identification.

"Four What-the-*F*s and one 'He looks like my uncle
Nicky from Sheepshead Bay.'" Ophelia checked
herself out in the mirror on the inside of the door to
the narrow coat closet. She wore a lime-green sweater
and black slacks, with hoop earrings as large as bracelets, and bracelets the length of necklaces, wound
around both wrists. They rattled when she patted her
freshly clipped Afro.

Far too pleased with herself, Marissa thought. *O must
know something good.* "Leaving…?"

"Leaving Marquese Griffin in accounting. He has a
crush on me."

"Does that mean he'll help?"

"He already has. The photo rang his bells, but he couldn't place the man, so he went through old files until he found the name to go with the face." Ophelia produced a note pad. "Hector Belbano, second vice president of Winter Industrial."

"Winter Industrial? Never heard of them." Marissa tapped keys to call up a roster of the firm's clients. "I'll see what I can find."

"Don't bother. Winter dumped us a year ago when they were bought out by one of those huge conglomerates with attorneys on twenty-four-hour tap."

"Then I'll run a search on Belbano. See what he's up to these days."

"Already did it." Ophelia flicked open her note pad. "And that's the most interesting thing. Belbano was 'removed' from the Winter payroll right after the buyout. I found nothing on him since. If he's employed, it's very discreetly, with a privately held business."

"Dead end." Marissa thumped her fist on the desk. "Unless we can get info directly from Paul." She cocked a brow at Ophelia. "Or his assistant?"

"Jodi Milbank." Ophelia shook her head. "The brain of a gnat. She'd run straight to Paul if I pried."

Marissa wasn't ready to give up. "How are you at creating a distraction?"

Ophelia rubbed her hands. The chunky gemstone bracelets clacked against each other. "Just point me in the right direction."

"Here's the plan. We watch for Paul to leave the office. Then you distract his assistant while I slip inside to see what I can find on Hector Belbano."

Ophelia seemed more than willing, but she hesitated. "Jamie wouldn't approve."

"How do you know?"

"He calls. We talk, we laugh. We share war stories."

"Not about me!"

"Watching after you is a full-time job," Ophelia said with fond indulgence. "Thank the Lord the boy is finally getting some compensation."

"Compensation," Marissa snorted, rushing O out of the office for a scouting mission. "Go see if Paul's working."

Ophelia pressed a hand to her rounded midriff. "Oh, I've got a pain in my side. Might be having me another of those gallbladder attacks any minute now. Right down the hall from sweet li'l helpful Jodi." She winked. "You be ready, boss."

14

OPHELIA'S GALLBLADDER got Jodi away from her seat and Marissa into Paul's office without a hitch. She went directly to the polished ebony desk and looked for an address or appointment book. Nothing. Damn his BlackBerry.

Checking the computer would be a wasted effort unless she had enough time to crack his log-in password. She sat, intending to try the desk, but there were no drawers except one so narrow and shallow only pens, a letter opener and a stash of Howard, Coffman letterhead fit inside. The notepad on the desk was blank, even when she held it to the light and looked for indentations.

She glanced around the office, desperate for any hint of life. Paul had no clutter. Some said a disorganized life was a sign of a scattered mind, but she chose to believe that an empty space indicated a lack of soul.

"Oh, oh, o-o-oh," Ophelia wailed from the hallway.

Marissa crossed to the file drawers built into the paneled wall. Every single one was locked.

"You'd think he had something to hide," she muttered.

She opened the coat closet, similar to her own. Inside

was a pair of polished wingtips, a rack of spare ties, a gray cashmere scarf. On the built-in shelf were two dress shirts, still in the Bergdorf's store wrapping.

Yep. All surface. No soul.

She turned away, her gaze falling on the telephone. Why not take a shot?

"I do believe I'm feeling better," Ophelia boomed from outside. Closer now. "If you'd just help me back to my desk, Jodi."

Panic spurted in Marissa: "Feeling better" was their code for Beware of Approaching Danger. Marissa had only seconds to spare. She could either get out of the office or pick up the phone.

She picked up the phone and hit the redial button.

After one ring, a male voice said, "McArdle."

She clamped her lips together, afraid that he'd hear her breathing.

"Beckwith?" the man asked with some suspicion. "You there?"

Marissa replaced the phone. She heard Jodi's lilting little-girl voice outside, answered by Paul's baritone.

Damn! She was stuck. The closet was too small, not to mention undignified. There was a couch, but it was backless, offering no possible hiding place.

With no choice but to brazen it out, Marissa darted across the room. She was standing by the window, admiring the view, when Paul entered. His face showed an instant of shock before he recovered and offered her a warm smile. "Hello, Marissa. How did you get past Jodi?"

"She wasn't at her desk."

He walked slowly around the room, his eyes sweeping the space, but she'd been meticulous in her search. Not a speck was out of place.

He sat, the smile almost gloating. "You've reconsidered."

"Reconsidered what?"

"Becoming a power couple. Ruling this firm."

"No."

His eyes narrowed. "Then what is it?"

She intended to go on the aggressive, but the phone rang before she could begin. Paul raised a finger to her and picked up.

A private line, she noticed, one that apparently bypassed Jodi's desk.

Paul watched Marissa coldly as his caller spoke. "Let me get back to you," he said, and hung up.

Her skin crawled. Was McArdle calling back after she hung up? She'd hoped he'd think Paul's phone had simply cut out.

She lengthened her neck, looking down on Paul with regal hauteur. "I came to ask if Mr. Howard had spoken to you."

Paul laughed without mirth, idly swinging from side to side in his swivel desk chair. "You thought you'd get a little revenge, is that it? Sorry to disappoint. Thomas saw your ploy for what it was, especially after I explained what a jealous lover you are."

She sucked in a cutting breath. "Do not think that I am as easy to fool," she seethed. "I know the woman from the beach has nothing to do with this."

Paul blinked. "With what?"

"The break-ins. The threats. The man you have spying on me."

"You've become paranoid. I have no one spying on you, Marissa."

Sure. "And the break-in? That wasn't an attempt to get the photos?"

Paul was so confident of his position that her accusations merely made him smile. "The photos have been destroyed."

She nodded as she edged toward the door. "So that's how it is."

Suddenly, Paul was up and across the room, pinching her by the shoulders, breathing hotly in her face. "You could have been a partner. You could have been with me."

She wrenched away. "Hard to decide which I want less," she snapped, and walked out of his office, thinking, *McArdle, McArdle.* She knew that name.

Ophelia was at her desk, chewing on a licorice stick when Marissa's memory banks kicked in. "Isn't one of the private investigators that the firm has on retainer named McArdle?"

"Ed McArdle," Ophelia said instantly. "You got a job for him? Are we hunting down Belbano?"

"Forget Belbano for now. Tell me what you know about McArdle."

"He's a tough customer. Ex-Marine, dishonorable discharge. The rumor around the lunchroom is that McArdle's the guy they call to handle touchy situations. Some say he's even known to lean on reluctant witnesses."

So much for the law firm's sterling reputation. Marissa's idols were crashing off pedestals all around her. She was rapidly reaching the point where if she could get out with an uncracked head, she'd count herself lucky.

Ophelia was watching Marissa's face. "You planning to clue me in?"

"You'll be the first to know, after Jamie." Marissa got a whiff of a strongly acrid scent as she walked by. "O, are you smoking again?"

The assistant made a guilty face. "I just sneaked one. All that moaning and wailing took it out of me. I don't know how Meryl Streep does it."

Marissa sniffed. Her senses were popping. "What kind of cigarettes do you smoke?"

"Newport. But I crushed all of mine during the big purge. I had to bum a ciggie from one of the paralegals. Terrible taste. Some pretentious brand she picked up when she went to Paris a month ago. Gauloises Blondes, I think she said. They're very strong."

"Paris." Marissa contemplated that, then shook her head. "The smell is naggingly familiar."

"Don't you mean gaggingly?" Ophelia shrugged. "Someone you know must smoke them."

"Must be," she mused, thinking of her tobacco-addicted stalker. The smell was the same, but why *French* cigarettes?

"I'm going back on the patch tomorrow," Ophelia promised.

"Good for you." Marissa meant that, but she was distracted by the latest piece of the puzzle. She suspected that if just one fell in place, the rest would follow. Jamie would say she should take her time, look over the entire picture before making the next move.

But that wasn't her way.

"WHAT'S UP?" Shandi said, throwing down her bag and dropping into the molded plastic chair opposite Jamie. He'd arranged to meet her at a coffee shop near his office, one that catered to a local clientele that ran in and out for coffee and sweets during the workday. Sisman was at the counter, hovering over the glass case of pastries as he selected his post-work doughnuts.

Shandi wrinkled her nose. "You said you need to interview me for an article?"

"I lied. That was just to get you here." He grabbed her wrist in case she tried to flee. "You're a hard person to get hold of."

"I'm busy. I've got stuff going on."

"What kind of stuff? Conspiring with Paul Beckwith perhaps?"

"Shit." She jerked her hand away. "You still on that? I haven't seen Paul in weeks and weeks."

Jamie went for shock tactics, to see how she'd react. "I know you slept with him."

"Oh, yeah? How do you know that?"

"I saw you two leave Mac's together, once upon a time."

She leaned her elbows on the table. "Guess what? You're not as smart as you think you are. Yeah, I talked to Paul. I even walked out with him. But I didn't go home with him. He tried for a piece, but I didn't go for it."

"I'm supposed to believe that?" Jamie searched Shandi's face, trying to look beneath the bravado and purple eye shadow.

"Believe me or not, I don't care." Her expression was pouty. She'd put a hand up to her hair and was twisting her corkscrew curls tighter and tighter around her fingers.

He shook his head, sure there was something she wasn't saying even if his assumptions about her hooking up with Paul had been wrong. "I'm sorry. I still don't think you're telling me everything."

She ran her teeth over her bottom lip. "It was always Marissa for you, wasn't it?"

"Yes."

"Okay. I'll lay it out for you." Shandi inhaled. "Never say I didn't do my bit for true love." She exhaled. "It's like this. When I was sleeping at Marissa's, y'know, right after she came home, I answered her cell and it was Paul. He tried to give me a line of crap, but the upshot was that he asked me to snoop around Marissa's place for some vacation photos she supposedly took. He said he'd pay me a couple of hundred bucks if I found them."

Shandi shifted nervously, avoiding Jamie's eyes. "I know it was a rotten thing to do, but I kinda needed the money, so I snooped. But I didn't find anything, and Paul had a screaming fit when I told him." She made a face. "There's something really wrong with that guy, if ya ask me."

"You should have told Marissa all of that as soon as you heard about the break-in."

"How was I supposed to know—"

"You knew. Guilt was all over your face."

"Maybe so." Shandi gulped. "Whatever. I tried to warn her, at least."

"'Watch your back,'" he said, repeating her warning. "Big help."

She scooted her chair back. "Are we through?"

"We're through."

"You'll be watching out for Marissa…?"

He crushed his paper coffee cup against the heel of his palm. Hot drops spattered. "Count on it."

MARISSA MET WITH a new client, studied an interrogatory pertaining to an ongoing lawsuit and stayed late researching Cayman Islands banking laws. She'd connected the dots between client cases that had required Ed McArdle's assistance, thanks to Ophelia's friend in payroll. Attorney of record on a disproportionate number of them: Paul Beckwith.

Interesting, but not totally illuminating.

She phoned Jamie, leaving voice mail when he didn't pick up. She'd had two messages from him, saying that she shouldn't go near Paul until they'd talked. Muttering about telephone tag, she reached under her desk to retrieve the pumps she'd kicked off an hour before. Her toes protested being stuffed back inside them, so she carried them in her hand as she picked up her Italian leather brief-bag and shut off the lights.

The offices were quiet, but not deserted. Too many of the lawyers worked late. The hum of vacuum cleaners testified to the cleaning staff's diligence.

Marissa walked on bare feet to the law library, where she dropped off a book on the librarian's desk. He got snippy if the lawyers didn't follow protocol about requesting and returning the volumes. She was heading out when she recognized two hushed voices.

Paul Beckwith and Thomas Howard. Coming in her direction.

She ducked back into the vast space of the law library, hurrying past the stately bookcases and threading through the more utilitarian banks of file cabinets without actually thinking where she was going.

The men had stopped directly outside the doorway. "I'm sure she was searching my office," Paul said. "She also called McArdle from my phone. He rang back when he got a hang-up from my number."

Marissa crouched, even though she was well hidden among the rows of cabinets that stretched to the ceiling. Her ears pricked as the conversation continued.

"What's she looking for?" Howard was clearly disgruntled. "You said you had her under your control, but first she sashays into my office with those damn photographs and now she's playing Nancy Drew. This is becoming more than an annoyance."

"She's nothing. She *knows* nothing."

Not wanting to miss a word, Marissa moved closer on silent feet, hugging her bag against her chest.

"Seems to me that she figured out that you had McArdle send that punk after her."

"But she doesn't know who Belbano is. That's what's important."

So tell me, she pleaded, but they weren't that stupid.

"She did surrender the photos without a fight," Howard said grudgingly.

"You'll have to give her a line about how you spoke to me."

"I'm the senior partner. I don't answer to her."

"No, sir." Marissa heard a shuffling sound. Paul must have moved because his voice lost volume. She inched closer, straining to hear. "We only have to placate her for the time being."

Howard grumbled.

"I know Marissa," Paul said. "She wants to keep her job a lot more than she wants to stick it to me. She's only being difficult because of her hurt pride."

Marissa's face grew hot. As much as she hated to admit it, there was a grain of truth in Paul's statement. The woman she'd been a few weeks ago might have been persuaded to put ambition above her ethics, if that only meant looking the other way.

But she'd changed.

She closed her eyes, silently thanking Jamie for widening her focus beyond her job and helping her to understand the value of keeping a good character. She'd do the right thing, but she wouldn't end up in a Miami storefront either.

"Then you should be the one to handle her. Either you make nice—" Howard's pause was punctuated by a *thump* against the door frame "—or you see that she stays out of our business. Permanently."

The ruthlessness from a man she'd trusted was too

much. With a gasp, Marissa bolted upright. The instinctive reaction almost made her drop her shoes and bag. She clutched at them, biting down on her tongue to keep from making another sound.

Thankfully, the men hadn't heard her. They moved away, breaking off the conversation and going in separate directions. After several minutes she crept to the doorway and peered along the corridor. Her heart was still pounding. Her mouth tasted like cotton.

The door to Paul's office was closed. She couldn't see Mr. Howard's spacious corner office from her vantage point.

She hesitated, contemplating the distance through the reception area and out the doors. Five seconds and she'd be free, if she ran. But strolling would look less suspicious. Either way, if they saw her, she was toast.

The hell with it. She ran.

Smack-dab into Jamie, coming through the doors from the other side.

15

"OH, THANK GOD, Jamie." Marissa practically collapsed into his arms, although she had enough sense to be sure that they ended up on the exterior side of the doors. "I've never been so glad to see you."

"What's going on?"

She threw him a quick hug, then pulled away to thrust her brief-bag into his arms. "Elevator first."

He punched the call button.

While waiting for the elevator to arrive, she hopped from one foot to the other, shoving her feet into her shoes. Jamie kept asking her what was wrong.

"Just hold on." She threw a nervous glance at the doors, fearing they'd open at any second. "I'll explain everything as soon as we're out of here."

Jamie also looked back. "I was coming to see Paul."

She blinked. "What for?"

"Uh. I was going to—"

"Beat him up for me?"

"Verbally, maybe. I thought it was time I confronted him head on. Put a stop to his harassment, and a few other things too."

"And so you made an appointment?" That was Jamie all over.

"Not really an appointment. I called, but he refused. So I came anyway. I figured at the end of the day, with less people around—"

She broke off the explanation. "Listen. After what I just overheard, that might not be a good idea. I've had quite an education."

"What do you mean?" He looked into her eyes and was alarmed by what he saw there. "You're scared."

She swallowed, but the words tumbled out anyway. "I made a big mistake going to Thomas Howard with my suspicions. Part of it was that I was trying to save my job, but I also thought that I could trust him to do the right thing. But he's involved in the scheme— whatever Paul did in the Caymans. I did get confirmation that they hired the burglar."

The elevator chime went off. The doors slid open. She stepped inside. Jamie did not.

"Come on! We have to go *now.*"

Just then Paul emerged from the office doors, looking pleased with himself until he saw Jamie and Marissa. His face darkened. "I told you I have nothing—"

He never got to finish. Jamie took him down with one well-placed blow to his perfect cleft chin.

Leaving Paul groaning on the floor, Jamie stepped into the elevator car. He shook his hand, as casually as if he played prize fighter every day before dinner. "Where to?"

This time Marissa didn't hesitate. "Take me to the police."

The sudden violence had startled her, especially coming from Jamie. But as they descended to safety, she decided that there was a great deal of ironic satisfaction in seeing Paul Beckwith fold like a cheap suit.

MARISSA PUT HER resignation in the mail the following morning. Then she sat on the sofa and looked around her apartment, trying to decide what to do. For the first time in ten—no, almost *fifteen* years, she had nothing to do.

Searching for another job could wait until Monday.

As much as she itched to call Ophelia to get the gossip from the office, she stopped herself. Guilty conscience, perhaps. Her decision to go to the police might result in innocent employees losing their jobs. O's position was almost certainly in jeopardy. If at all possible, Marissa would employ her friend in her next position.

If she got one.

She jiggled her foot. Her nails bit into her palms. Future employment was debatable, especially after the word got out that she'd become a whistleblower.

The police hadn't been overly impressed with either her tale of skullduggery at the law firm or the photographic evidence. A daunting white-collar crime to investigate, they'd said—and off-shore, too—especially when no one knew if there'd really been a crime. Officer O'Connor had promised to notify the proper authorities, which could include the IRS, the New York State bar association, even the Feds, if her suspicions of embezzlement or money laundering were true.

The cops' first cursory check on Belbano had revealed not only that he had a record of embezzlement, but that he'd made frequent trips to the Caymans in the past two years. Whether he was employed by one of the firm's clients, or even by the partnership itself, remained a mystery for now.

The officers had brightened when she'd given them the private investigator's name as the link between the thug Freddy Bascomb and Howard, Coffman, Ellis and Schnitzer. Even if the other investigation went nowhere, it was almost certain they would find evidence of complicity in the breaking and entering of her apartment. Perhaps even of Bascomb's murder.

McArdle had been brought in for immediate questioning. Inevitably, the trail would reach Paul and the partners, particularly if Shandi agreed to give a statement about how Paul had asked her to snoop.

Marissa winced. The partners would be enraged with her for turning over the evidence. Even Shandi might be a reluctant witness.

Stop beating yourself up. The forthcoming mess at the law firm was not her fault. Nor Paul's, entirely.

Thomas Howard was ultimately to blame, and any of the other partners who were involved. She sincerely hoped they were not. Other concerns aside, she was appalled that Mr. Howard had used a false paternal relationship to fool her into believing he was a man she could trust.

She'd been so sure of herself, so set in her path, that she'd badly misstepped along the way.

Thank heaven for Jamie. She smiled, just thinking about how he'd punched Paul in the jaw then swept her off to the police station. The boy next door had grown up and become the man she'd been looking for.

Something unique and wonderful had happened between them. She couldn't say how or why, beyond there being a vague sense of destiny involved.

Harry walked in and cocked his head at Marissa. The tip of his tail twitched. She recognized the signs—he wanted to jump into her lap. Was probably only hesitating because it was so unusual to find her at home during the day, sitting and doing nothing.

Enough thinking! She stood with a, "Sorry, Harry." Suddenly she knew what she had to do: clean house.

She'd already begun, clearing out and fumigating the closet after Harry had used it for a litter box. Now she wanted to continue, to sweep all her old junk out and make way for a fresh, new life. She wasn't going to transform into an uber-housewife, that was for sure, but she needed to make a positive start on the future.

The kitchen was in pretty good shape, so she made a pass through the living room, bundling up magazines and mail-order catalogs for recycling, dusting the electronics, fishing out the items that Harry had batted beneath the bookshelves. She washed windows. Vacuumed up cat hair. Then went on to scrub the bathroom.

She moved to the bedroom, followed by Harry, whipping his tail in agitation. Since the closet was clean, she started under the bed, pulling out various items until she got to the empty suitcase. Her carry-on bag fit inside. She went to push them back under the bed.

Bad mojo.

She'd kept her bags packed, figuratively speaking, throughout every relationship of her life, even when it came to how fervently she'd wanted to get away from her father. This time, with Jamie, she'd do it right.

Feeling slightly silly, she carried the suitcases to the closet, stretching on her toes to place them on the top shelf. They tilted precariously, canted on her fingertips. She rose higher. One more inch.

Harry yowled from his perch on the radiator. She lost balance and dropped onto her heels, the suitcase coming down on top of her. It glanced off her head and thudded to the floor. The flap popped open.

"Crap." Marissa knelt to zip it up. Beneath the bed, a small white object caught her eye. She reached for it. A piece of jewelry. "Where did this come from?"

Not your average necklace, she saw immediately. It appeared to be antique—a piece of ivory carved in the shape of a star. At first she was almost leery to touch it, poking at the piece with only one finger. She realized that she was holding her breath.

The pure white star was too lovely to resist. She picked up the fragile treasure, studying it in the palm of her hand. The ivory was set in gold with a hollow at the center.

So beautiful. She wanted to string it as a necklace and wear it for Jamie.

Marissa cupped it against her chest. The piece was tucked in her palm, the fit so precise, the feel so right that she wished she could keep it forever.

But she couldn't. The star wasn't hers.

What was it doing under her bed, hidden by the bag? Could it have fallen out of the suitcase?

The trip to the Caymans, she thought, remembering how she'd joked about discovering that she'd smuggled in a valuable item. *¡Dios mio! Had she?*

But the burglar had been after the photos. Paul had admitted as much.

Marissa opened her hand. Warmed by her skin, the star seemed to glow. It had to be rare. Valuable. She must get it evaluated by a professional. And find the rightful owner.

But for now, she owned it, at least for a little while. Why not try it on?

She found a ribbon and threaded it through the small hole in the star, then slipped the necklace over her head. After she'd pulled her hair away from her neck, the star came to rest just below the hollow in her throat.

She went to look in the mirror, taken with the timeless beauty of the piece.

She'd wear it tonight, she decided. *For Jamie, the man I love.*

HE'D EXPECTED that she would have crashed by now, the reality of her situation hitting home like the crack of a baseball bat. But no. She opened the door, smiling and beautiful in a sleeveless white dress that skimmed her body from a scooped neck that showed off the tops of her breasts to a hem that ended inches above her bare feet. Her hair was up in a neat little braided knot.

"Quitting your job seems to agree with you."

"Oh, that," she said airily, lifting and cocking her head.

He thought she wanted him to kiss her cheek, so he did. She gave off a fragrant warmth, like a woman fresh from an exotically spiced and scented bath. His constant desire for her flared higher.

Her lips were puckered. Her eyes were large, expectant, framed in thick black lashes and a stroke of smoky color. He sensed she was waiting for him to comment, like a woman with a new hairstyle.

His eyes swept her, lingering over her sleek curves, but stopping on the necklace.

He stared, slow to comprehend because he'd only glanced at the Sisman's story in the paper.

Damn. Did she know?

She stroked her collarbone. "What do you think? Do I do it justice?"

He nodded.

"I *found* it. Under my *bed*. When I was *cleaning*." She laughed, twirling on her bare feet like a young girl. "Unbelievable! All of it."

"Do you know what that is?"

"The necklace?"

"The White Star," he said.

She faltered. "What are you talking about?"

"Did you hear about the auction house theft from a while back? Skip Sisman's been covering the story for the *Village Observer*. One of the stolen items was the White Star amulet."

"You can't think this is *the* White Star!"

He shrugged. "Looks like it to me."

"Oh, come on." She twisted her neck, trying to look at it. "How can you tell?"

"Well, I could be wrong. For sure, I'm no expert." He remembered the newspaper folded under his arm and shook it out. "Today's edition. They finally ran Sisman's update on the theft, with a sidebar on the history of the amulet." He folded open the paper, stopping twice to stare at the alluring ivory star around her neck. It caught the eye. "That's got to be it. The freaking White Star!"

She touched it tentatively. "That's crazy. I found it in my suitcase."

He handed her the paper. "Take a look."

She examined a grainy black-and-white photo that accompanied the article, a thirty-year-old shot of an heiress wearing the amulet to a society party. "I'll concede that there's an obvious similarity. Both amulets are the same shape, of course, but this photo isn't clear enough to make out the details. I'm probably wearing a knock-off version."

"Do you really believe that?"

"I'm not sure." She touched the star's face. "The quality is too fine and, well, this might sound preposterous, but it *feels* real."

"And you found it in your suitcase?"

"No, the star was under the bed. I saw it after I moved the bag. I think it had fallen from an outside pocket."

"When Shandi searched your belongings for Paul."

"Maybe. There's no way of being certain how or when it happened. I just know that I had no idea I was carrying a valuable amulet."

Jamie spoke slowly in disbelief. "Someone else must have put it in your bag."

"Could it have been Paul?"

"I don't see it."

"Me, neither," she agreed. "For one thing, the burglar he hired would have known exactly where to look." She returned to the article in the paper. "They're speculating the amulet is from an ancient African civilization," she mused. "Three thousand years old! Incredible."

"Stolen property. We have to call the police."

"They must be sick of me by now. Can't you just see O'Connor's face when I tell him *this* story?" She touched the amulet again, unable to resist even though she knew she should take it off immediately. Just in case. "I thought that I'd get an expert's opinion first and then…" She sighed.

"You don't want to give it up."

Nodding. "I'd keep it forever if I could."

"You look like a desert princess. Your skin, your eyes, the black hair."

She came into his arms, crumpling the newspaper between them. "I feel so…oh, I don't know. Different."

He played with a loose tendril of her hair, curling it against her pinkened cheek. "Different how?"

"I can't explain. If I was the mystical woo-woo type of girl, I'd swear it's the amulet. As if it has a special power." She gave a skeptical laugh, but he could tell that some part of her believed what she'd said. "Whatever's happening, I know that I'm more sure than I've ever been."

"Sure of what?"

She blushed. "Of you and me. How much I love you."

His heart might have stopped. Or maybe it was time that did. The rotation of the earth, the ocean tide. Something—anything—to mark this moment of pure joy.

"I love you," he said, gently tilting her face for his kiss. The difference was there, too, a covenant that flowed between them like a river rushing into a waterfall. Sweeping them up, carrying them away.

They held each other for a long while, sharing soft kisses and sweet words, woven in the promise and power of love. He felt as if he could conquer the world.

Reluctantly she pulled away. "I should take this off, on the chance that it is genuine," she said, stroking the ribbon. "The amulet's probably very fragile."

He followed her into the bedroom, smoothing and folding the newspaper before tossing it onto the bed. Her hands lifted to remove the necklace, but he said, "Wait." Stunned by her beauty. "Let me look at you."

Smiling, she lowered her arms. "Take your hair down," he said.

She undid the bun, the braid, shaking her hair across

her shoulders in a rippled ebony wave. "There's a look in your eye," she said. Her lips puckered into a kiss that he swore he felt from across the room. "What do you have in mind?"

As if she didn't know. He was brimming with lust. "Wear the amulet." Each word was distinct and separate and momentous. "Only for tonight."

Her expression showed her inner struggle. "I can't." Reluctantly she removed the necklace and laid it carefully on the bedside table. "If it's real, it must be worth a lot of money." She turned to him. "Do you still want me without it?"

"As if there's a question."

She smiled, her bare arms curving into an invitation.

He pulled the lace curtains. The light diffused, throwing spangled lacy patterns across Marissa's white dress and golden skin.

Savoring the moment, he approached slowly. She waited, her hands clasped. Different, yes, she was different. Patient and still. But also the same. The woman he knew so well that she'd become a part of him.

He slid the dress off her shoulders, kissing each inch of skin as it was revealed. Her nape, her back, her shoulders, her breasts. The garment fell away, pooling around her feet. He knelt, slowly peeling away her underpants. His fingers brushed across her hipbone, the flare of her hips, her legs like slender stems. His lips followed the same path. He breathed deeply, tantalized by her scent.

He glanced at the amulet. There was something fascinating about it, almost otherworldly. He sensed its power, even though ten minutes ago he would have scoffed in disbelief that such a thing might be true.

Marissa had begun to tremble. He scooped her up,

laid her on the bed that had been stripped to its sheets. She sighed and relaxed, stretching out her arms so her hands dangled off the sides of the bed. Her face was serene. A goddess, giving herself over to a higher power, surrendering to fate.

He forgot about the amulet. Marissa, pure and bare and true, was fascinating enough for him.

Her lashes fluttered. A small smile appeared. "Don't just stand there. Make love to me."

That was her, all the way. He was almost relieved.

"As you wish, goddess." He removed his clothing, letting the potency wash through him as she gazed at him with equal awe. There had been times he'd wondered if he was really the right man—enough man—for her, but now he knew. He felt it.

They would be together forever.

He lowered himself, taking her mouth first. She was sweet and fresh. Then her neck, the smooth skin of her shoulders. Her arms. He kissed the inside of her elbow and she sighed and wiggled her hips, nestling his erection against her flat belly. So hot and slick down there that he shuddered.

"Love you, babe." He nuzzled at her breast. She shifted, sweeping her hands along his back in a luxurious stroke. Her fingers worked through his hair and she pressed, directing his mouth to her nipple. He teased it with his tongue, then suckled.

Her legs spread. He felt the honeyed heat of her like a magnet, inexorably drawing him in. The first thrust went deep and she flung back her head, her arms and legs flying in every direction as she was pinioned. Other times, he would have slowed, but his instincts were driving and she was squeezing down on him and he needed to be there, at the throbbing heart of her, where they merged into one.

They moved together, passion and pleasure becoming a molten flow. His blood pounded. She cried his name, holding nothing back.

Their climax was transporting. Transcending.

Then it was over, and they were utterly spent, gasping for breath as they floated back to earth. Even when their breathing quieted, there were no words that sufficed. He satisfied himself with holding her within the shelter of his crossed arms, counting the beats of her heart beneath his palm.

"You felt it, too," she whispered.

"God, yes."

"The amulet."

"I don't know." He closed his eyes. "Yes."

She said no more.

He kissed the back of her shoulder.

Her butt snuggled into spooning position. Paper crackled. She kicked a foot. "I'll get it," he said, reaching down to fling away the newspaper.

"Wait." She plucked it from his hand. "I want to see the photo again. In my heart, I know that we have the amulet, but the cynical part of me says there's no way it should be."

"Love is a mystery. But I always knew there'd come a day for us. It's the lace and flowers."

She rattled the paper. "What lace and flowers?"

"In this bedroom. You're a closet romantic."

"Um."

"I'm wrong?"

"I sublet this apartment, remember? The woman who

had it before me was the one who decorated. If I ever get around to changing the decor, I'll have Spanish tiles and white plaster walls with a bed made of bamboo. No lace. No flowers."

"Oh." He was taken aback for a moment or two. Then he threw back his head and laughed heartily. The joke was on him, but he didn't care. Her heart had revealed itself, regardless of her preference in curtains.

She rolled onto her stomach to study the paper. "I don't see what's so darn—huh." She gripped the page between her hands. "Wait…I know him!"

"Who?"

"This guy. This one." She'd sat up and was stabbing the paper excitedly. "I recognize him from the airport."

"Jean Luc Allard," Jamie read. Sisman's article delved into possible suspects in the Stanhope theft. They were identified by picture and name. Allard's photo was a distant street shot, fuzzily enlarged and cropped on his face. "Are you sure? The photo stinks."

"It looks like him. And he's French." Marissa bounced the heel of her palm off her head. "Of course. The cigarettes. The smell has been haunting me. He reeked of them at the airport and then—" She blinked. "Oh, my God. *Allard* is the one who's been following me. He's the smoker. And that must have been *him* at the bottom of the fire escape!"

"Wait a minute. If this Allard stole the White Star, how did it wind up in your bag?"

"He must have put it there. A woman bumped into me, and I fell, and he picked up my passport, I remember that. There's your opportunity."

"But why would he do it? If you'd been leaving the country, sure, he might use you to smuggle the amulet out. But you were returning."

"Yeah, you have a point." She frowned, thinking. "Okay, here's the thing. There were a lot of guards and police around that day. If Allard thought they were going to pick him up, he might have wanted to ditch the amulet any way he could. In my bag. And since he looked at my passport, he got my address. So he could watch me." She crowed. "That's it!"

"Could be."

"He tried to get it back. Coming home, remember? The mugger who went for my suitcase."

"What about Freddy Bascomb? Were they working together?"

"I doubt it. Paul has no connection to the amulet."

"Bascomb was stabbed…"

"Two blocks away." She went white. "If Allard was keeping an eye on me all this time, he might have thought that Bascomb had taken the amulet."

"This is making a weird kind of sense."

"All those times I thought I was being watched," she mused. "It was him. In the lobby, on the street—" She arched her brows at the barred window. "Probably even on my fire escape."

"So we can't blame all of it on Paul," Jamie said, frowning.

"There's enough blame to go around." Marissa picked up the paper again. "At least now we know what's been going on. After the White Star is out of our hands, life will go back to normal."

"Will it?" Jamie asked. *Do you want it to?*

"You know what I mean." She threw the paper aside

and curled up beside him. "Here's what we'll do. In the morning, I'll call my friend Trish. Her brother, Alex, works at an antiquities museum. We'll have one of their experts take a look at the amulet to be sure it's the original before we go to the authorities. That'll save us some embarrassment in case we find out it's a fake."

"It's not a fake."

"Ah, yes, Allard," she said, resting her chin on his chest. "Of course."

"Allard's not the proof."

Marissa's eyes met his. She was beginning to smile. A complex, knowing, slightly mysterious smile. The smile of an exotic goddess who'd captured his heart.

"*This* is the proof," he said, reaching an arm past her as if he were going for the White Star on the nearby table.

His hand landed on her shoulder instead. Her brows rose with a question.

A question answered when he took her mouth in a kiss that was all the testament either of them needed.

Epilogue

SPRING SUNSHINE splashed across the pavement. The leaves of the chestnut trees shimmied, flipping from light to dark and back to light with the turn of the breeze. Allard paced, wishing for the night though he knew that his chance would come in daylight.

There might be only one chance. He had to be vigilant.

The waiting and watching had taken their toll. He was restless, jumpy. His instincts hummed. Every noise from the apartment building made him twitch with anticipation.

He was on the other side of the street, lighting a cigarette in the shadow of a double-parked delivery truck when the door of the brownstone opened and Marissa emerged. Too late for work—a worrying detail. Accompanied by her troublesome boyfriend.

Allard pinched the cigarette from his mouth. Something was wrong.

She wore jeans and a clingy sweater, with a leather bag strapped across her chest, cradled in protective hands. The boyfriend was scanning the street. He hustled her toward a cab that had pulled up to the curb.

Allard tossed away the cigarette and sprinted across

the street, coming within reach of their vehicle as it pulled away. He knew…he knew…

Allard whistled for a passing cab that didn't stop. He ran it down, swearing in French as he saw the other cab signal for a turn. They were heading uptown.

He threw himself into the car, told the cabbie to floor it.

He couldn't lose them!

They had the White Star. Even without the clues, he would have seen it in her eyes.

His greatest fear was that they were going to the police. His employer would never tolerate that.

But after a harried ride through traffic, they stopped outside a large gray edifice with Doric columns and tall windows capped by carved lintels. The letters etched above the columns read: Museum of Antiquities.

Allard's pulse raced in step with the pair as they flew from the cab and up the stone staircase. Attempting a chase was not necessary. He'd accessed museums before, and would do it again, in a ploy more clever than running through the streets in broad daylight.

The White Star could change hands a dozen times over, but her fate would never be altered.

His were the hands she wanted—quick, skilled, secretive.

His were the hands she'd get.

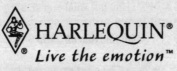

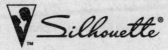

HARLEQUIN®

Blaze™

COMING NEXT MONTH

#237 ONCE UPON A SEDUCTION Jamie Sobrato
It's All About Attitude

He's *so* not Prince Charming. Otherwise Nico Valetti wouldn't be causing all these problems for Skye Ellison. Not the least of which is the fact that she can't keep her hands off him. And since she is traveling in a car with him for days on end, seducing him will just be a matter of time.

#238 BASIC TRAINING Julie Miller

Marine Corps captain Travis McCormick can't believe it when Tess Bartlett—his best friend and new physiotherapist—asks for basic training in sex. Now that he's back in his hometown to recover from injuries, all he wants is a little R & R. Only, Tess has been working on a battle plan for years, and it's time to put it to work. She'll heal him...if he'll make *her* feel all better!

#239 WHEN SHE WAS BAD... Cara Summers
24 Hours: Island Fling, Bk. 3

P.I. Pepper Rossi had no intention of indulging in an island fling. She's at the romantic island resort simply to track down a priceless stolen painting. Only, with sexy ex-CIA agent Cole Buchanan dogging her every step, all she can think about is getting him off her trail...and into her bed!

#240 UP ALL NIGHT Joanne Rock
The Wrong Bed

Devon Baines can't resist the not-so-innocent e-mail invitation. And once he spies Jenny Moore wearing just a little bit of lace, he doesn't care that he wasn't the intended recipient. Sparks fly when these two insomniacs keep company after midnight!

#241 NO REGRETS Cindi Myers

A near-death experience has given her a new appreciation of life. As a result, Lexie Foster compiles a list of things not to be put off any longer. The first thing on her list? An affair with her brand-new boss, Nick Delaney. And convincing him will be half the fun.

#242 CAUGHT Kristin Hardy
The White Star, Bk. 3

With no "out" and no means to reach the outside world, Julia Covington and Alex Spencer are well and truly caught! Trapped in a New York City antiquities museum by a rogue thief isn't the way either one anticipated spending the weekend, but now that it's happened... What will become of the stolen White Star, the charmed amulet Julia is meant to be researching? And what *won't* they do to amuse one another as the hours tick by?

www.eHarlequin.com

HBCNM0206